THE BOUNTY HUNTER

Bounty hunter Orrin Reed never goes after a man who doesn't deserve to die or be put away, never targets anyone about whom there is any question of guilt, never pursues a person whose crime could possibly have been justified. After Nate Niedermeyer slips through his fingers, Orrin trails him into the wilderness and takes him prisoner. But the river rages high and wild, friends of Nate are riding to his rescue, and the scattered forest provides inadequate cover. Can Orrin escape these deadly straits, or is he doomed?

BILLY HALL

◆

THE BOUNTY HUNTER

Complete and Unabridged

LINFORD
Leicester

First published in Great Britain in 2015 by
Robert Hale Limited
London

First Linford Edition
published 2016
by arrangement with
Robert Hale
an imprint of The Crowood Press
Wiltshire

A catalogue record for this book is available
from the British Library.

ISBN 978–1–4448–3043–9

Published by
F. A. Thorpe (Publishing)
Anstey, Leicestershire

Set by Words & Graphics Ltd.
Anstey, Leicestershire
Printed and bound in Great Britain by
T. J. International Ltd., Padstow, Cornwall

This book is printed on acid-free paper

1

It was a gamble. The only thing at stake was his life.

The frigid wind swept down the rock-hard, frozen street of Serenity, Wyoming. Though the wind was at his back, its icy fingers probed through every gap in his clothing. It shuddered between his neckerchief and hat. It pushed in uneven gusts against him, keeping him from standing as still as he would have liked.

His long riding coat was pulled back, held away from the tied-down Colt .45 by his gloved left hand that reached around behind him. His right hand had no such protection. It was that which provided his dilemma.

There were those who wore a tight, kid-leather glove on their gun hand. It helped a little. It didn't really help all that much against this kind of cold. It did slow down a man's ability to draw and shoot in a hurry.

On the other hand, so did the cold. 'Thermometer says she's ten below zero,' the bartender had announced half an hour ago.

The rushing wind magnified that temperature's effect on any unprotected flesh. Like a gun hand. In seconds it made the fingers tangibly stiff. That slowed the speed of a draw. It also affected the feel of the gun in the hand that controlled the aim.

That's why his right hand was still inside the coat, spread against the left side of his rib cage, way too far away from his gun. But it was warm there. If he were able to gauge the right moment to withdraw that hand from its cosy shelter, he would have a warm hand with which to draw. If he withdrew it too soon, it would become cold and stiffen perceptibly. Either mistake would cost him his life.

Before him, thirty feet away, Leo Toczek faced him. Leo was among the men Orrin Reed had been pursuing across Kansas, across a corner of Colorado, into Wyoming Territory. Leo was a wanted man. There was a price on his head. A substantial price. It was there for good reason. A more than substantial reason.

Orrin well knew the details. He always studied the details. He asked a lot of questions. He was a bounty hunter. He knew well that was a dirty word. He was determined never to fall into the habit of others who plied his profession of thinking only of the bounty. He never went after a man who didn't deserve to die or to be put away in prison for a good long time. He never targeted anyone about whom there was any question of guilt. He eschewed pursuit of anyone whose crime he deemed as possibly being justified.

He had nearly made that mistake once. He had learned his quarry's newly assumed identity. He had hunted him to ground. He had braced him, told him he was under arrest, ordered him to throw up his hands. The man had asked to be heard before bullets flew. He readily confessed to hunting down the man he had killed. He just as readily confessed to shooting him as he would a rabid dog. He also disclosed that the man he killed had raped his very young daughter. The local sheriff had refused to do anything about it, citing the unsubstantiated testimony of the girl as the only evidence.

The man had offered the names of those in the town he had fled as references of his truthfulness. He had also offered his word to stay where he had homesteaded if Orrin took the time to check out his story.

Feeling like a gullible dupe, Orrin had actually agreed to do so. It had taken almost two weeks for telegrams to be sent and received from those whose testimony had been offered. A telegram from the sheriff there finally corroborated his refusal to pursue the charges against the man. Everything the man had told him checked out.

The man had fled with his family, changed his name, homesteaded under that new name, and was a well-respected member of the area. So far as he knew, Orrin was the only person who had managed to connect him to the crime, and learn his new name. That knowledge had ridden away with Orrin. He had filed the only deliberately false report he had ever filed. He had sent notice to the sheriff in question that the fugitive was rumoured to have fled to South America, and that his wife had remarried.

The man who faced him today had no such story to tell, had he tried to tell one. Orrin checked things out much more carefully, since that near miscarriage of justice. He knew beyond doubt that Leo Toczek was guilty of several murders, a number of robberies, and other malefactions. He also knew Leo was fast with a gun. Very fast.

'Unbuckle your gunbelt and toss it down, Leo,' he ordered. 'You're out of anywhere to run.'

Leo laughed a sharp one-syllable bark. 'I didn't walk out here in this weather to surrender to some bounty hunter. Go for it whenever you're ready to die.'

Moving slowly, Orrin moved his hand from its pocket of warmth. He had noted with some small satisfaction that Leo had been standing for several minutes with his ungloved hand poised right at his gun butt. 'His hand oughta be good and cold,' Orrin thought. 'Might be edge enough.'

Somewhere up the street, the incessant wind managed to rip a board loose from the eave of a building. It bowed out and slapped back against the eave with a bang. As if that were a signal, both men grabbed their guns. Two pistols whipped upward with lightning speed. Two shots resounded down the empty street the barest instant apart.

The wind chose that moment to pause, as if even it held its breath. Then it whipped at the frozen vista with renewed force. As if blown from his feet by that renewed blast, Leo fell backward, spread-eagled on the ground. As he landed, one foot jerked into the air and fell back. A tumbleweed the wind had dislodged rolled down the street. Because even it was frozen stiff and brittle, it left some of itself behind every time it contacted the ground. By the time it exited the other end of the town's main street, it was half the size it had been when it entered.

Orrin holstered his weapon. He shuddered once, but whether from the icy wind or from another brush with death was uncertain. He pulled the long coat closed and buttoned a couple of buttons to keep it there. From a pocket he pulled a heavy, lined glove that matched the one on his other hand. He pulled it on to his gun hand with a rush of relief.

People along the street peered from windows, loathe to step outside unless it was entirely necessary. A couple of doors opened briefly and faces appeared before they were hurriedly closed again. Whether against the cold or the maca-bre scene in the street was one more uncertainty.

Orrin strode to the town marshal's office to file the necessary paperwork. The wages for which he had placed his life on the line today would bolster his nest egg nicely.

2

'You ain't aimin' to hang around long, I don't 'spect.'

Orrin eyed the town marshal carefully, trying to read his body language. 'I ain't in any hurry to leave,' he said. 'Why?'

Marshal Clive Missner spat a brown stream more or less into the spittoon beside his desk. 'Most folks ain't too comfortable havin' a bounty hunter hangin' around.'

Orrin's eyes flashed briefly. It was one of those conversations that carried with it the sense of having been here before, having heard all the same words, seen all the same disdain in others' eyes. Usually he ignored it. Maybe the bitterly cold weather affected his mood. Maybe the marshal's slovenly appearance and apparent laziness just irritated him more than usual.

For whatever reason, he answered it.

'Does anyone feel that way besides the law officer that should've had a flyer about a wanted man that was living openly in his town and should've already done something about it himself?'

The marshal wasn't fazed. If his manhood or his work ethic had been challenged, he didn't seem to care. 'He wasn't botherin' me any,' he tossed back. 'As long as he didn't cause any trouble in my town, what he mighta did somewheres else ain't no skin off my backside.'

'Are you afraid havin' a bounty hunter in town might put some o' that hide in danger?'

Missner actually chuckled. 'The only thing I worry about is havin' to lock up a drunk cowboy once in a while till he sobers up. That an' keepin' a lid on things in town. If you wanta shake the bushes an' see if you can find some other fella that's got a couple dollars on his head, you just go right ahead. One of 'em'll beat you to the draw one o'these days. Either that or, more likely, shoot ya outa the saddle afore ya even know he's around. Then you won't be near so high'n mighty.'

Orrin swallowed the retort that was pushing to escape his restraint. Instead he said, 'I'd be plumb happy if you'd just take care o' the paperwork on Toczek. As soon as Dickinson County wires me the money I got comin', I'll be movin' on.'

'Where's Dickinson County? I ain't never heard of it.'

'Kansas.'

Missner grunted. 'What part o' Kansas?'

'Abilene.'

'Huh. That figgers. Seems to be fertile ground for growin' bad apples. That's where Hardin came from, as I remember.'

'Uh huh.'

Missner stood. 'All right. I'll get the paperwork done an' the wire sent. I'll let ya know when I hear somethin'.

You'll be stayin' at the hotel, I 'spect.'

Orrin almost smiled. 'Yeah. Unless you're just dyin' for me to stay in your guest room at home instead.'

The marshal didn't quite smile, but it was the closest Orrin had seen to one on the dour lawman. 'If I had a guest room, I'd have to figger out a way to tell you that you wasn't welcome. Sort of a good thing for your tender feelin's that I ain't got one.'

'Well, I guess I'll just have to wander over to the Silver Dollar an' drown my disappointment.'

'They burn coal.'

The comment seemed to make no sense to Orrin. 'What?'

'They burn coal. The Silver Dollar. They got three stoves, an' vents what open to the rooms upstairs so's the heat gets up there too. But they don't burn wood. Same with the hotel. Here where we got more deadfall layin' in the timber all around us than we can use, they burn coal. The Silver Dollar an' the hotel both freight in a couple or three wagon loads o' coal from down at Rock Springs 'stead o' havin' to cut wood or buy it.'

'Burns hotter, I'm told.'

'Does for a fact. Them stoves get plumb red hot when she gets down around thirty below. Lot less ashes to deal with, too.'

'Sure's dirty stuff to handle, though.'

'The ones what stoke 'em keep a pair o' gloves just for that. They still end up blacker'n the ace o' spades. I'll just stick to good firewood.'

It was closer to a civil conversation than Orrin had expected, considering his first impression of the man. He pondered the reason for his sudden loquaciousness as he stepped out the door.

The wind slammed its frigid fist into him the instant he stepped outside. He ducked his head, grabbing his hat to keep it from flying away. Leaning into the force of the gale, he walked catercorner across the street. He stepped through the door of the Silver Dollar and quickly closed it behind himself.

His eyes swept the large room in a swift arc. Nearly a dozen round tables were spread evenly through the back half of the room. Three large pool tables occupied the area nearest to the front wall. Between the two halves of the room, three large cast iron stoves emitted copious amounts of welcome heat.

Perpendicular to the rows of tables and stoves, a large bar ranged from the front wall to the back. One section of that bar was hinged to lift upward. It provided the only access to the area behind it. The shelves on the back wall held an impressive array of spirits. Keeping watch over them, the oversized picture of a reclining nude woman seemed to invite the saloon's patrons to pay for the privilege of lifting the dingy piece of red material that offered the only concession to her modesty.

Orrin shrugged out of the heavy drover's long-coat. He hung it from one of the hooks on the long rack extending along the wall beside the front door. He pushed his hat to the back of his head, but spurned any thought of hanging it with the coat.

As he bellied up to the bar the bartender was already there waiting for him. 'What'll it be?'

'Got a good bourbon that ain't watered?'

'I don't water my whiskey. I do have the best sour mash you'll find in Wyoming Territory. All the way from Tennessee. Jack Daniels.'

'Never heard of it.'

'Best there is, for my money.'

'I'll take your word for it.'

He tossed a coin on the bar. The bartender picked a bottle from the back wall and poured a shot from it into the glass he set in front of Orrin.

Orrin picked it up and sipped it carefully. He held it in his mouth a long moment, then swallowed. He exhaled slowly, enjoying the glow as it spread from his stomach, driving the cold from him. He nodded appreciatively. 'Well, I don't know if you're a gentleman or a scholar, but you are a fine judge of whiskey,' he complimented the bartender.

The bartender nodded his thanks. 'Want me to leave the bottle?'

Orrin shook his head. 'No, thanks. One's my limit.'

'Good idea for a man in your line of work.'

Orrin smiled tightly. 'My reputation precedes me.'

'Most fellas' does, in this country. Ain't a whole lot to do 'cept work, drink and gossip.'

'And not everyone works or drinks, but everyone gossips.'

The bartender extended a hand. 'I'm Butch, by the way.'

Orrin took the hand and returned the strong grip. 'Orrin Reed. Happy to make the acquaintance of someone that doesn't think bounty hunters are two notches lower'n a snake's belly.'

'Good share of 'em are.'

Orrin savoured another sip of the

whiskey. Butch spread his hands wide and leaned on the bar, studying Orrin for a long moment. Finally he said, 'Too bad you ain't after the other one too.'

Orrin's attention snapped to alert status instantly. 'Other one?'

There was the barest moment of hesitation before the barkeep answered. 'Friend o' Toczek's. He lives along the crick 'bout ten miles north. He's a loner. My guess is that he's a wanted man, too. Meaner'n Toczek, especially if he's had a drink or two. Him an' Toczek usually disappear about the same time and show up again about the same time, flush with money again. They don't neither one work for anybody that I know of.'

'What's he look like?'

'Big man. Couple inches over six foot. Dark brown eyes. Real dark. Black hair. Full beard any time I ever seen 'im. Got a scar down along the left side of his face. Looks like a knife scar. Barely missed his eye.'

Orrin's forehead knit thoughtfully. He turned and walked over to where his coat hung on the wall. He dug through an inside pocket a long moment and returned to the bar. He unfolded a well-worn piece of paper, exposing a faded wanted poster.

'That him?'

'That's him, sure as sin,' Butch replied. 'Howard Dubray, huh? Goes by the name Harold Danson around here. Five hundred and twenty-five dollar reward, dead or alive. Now that's a real odd amount for a bounty on a man, ain't it?'

Orrin nodded. 'Only one I've ever seen like it. They usually favour round numbers. Ten miles north, huh?'

Butch nodded. 'All you gotta do is follow the crick. When it splits about six or seven miles up, follow the west fork of it. Ain't that much of a place. Got a decent cabin an' sort of a barn for the horses. Does have some fine horses. Usually three or four. Otherwise there ain't no sign of any sort o' work gettin' done, 'cept just enough hayin' to get his horses through the winter. Like Toczek, he comes to town once a month or so.'

Warning bells had been jingling in Orrin's mind since the bartender had begun the conversation. It wasn't totally out of place, but certainly unusual. He decided to put his concerns into words.

'So what've you got against the man?'

Butch's head jerked up. 'What d'ya mean?'

'Seems sorta odd you just happen to bring him up to a bounty hunter you've never met before.'

The bartender took a deep breath. 'There's some men the country'd be better off without. Worse than the ones from Foster's Hole. I 'specially got no time for woman beaters.'

'Woman beaters?'

Butch pointed with his chin. 'See the red-headed woman over by the back wall?'

Orrin turned around and hooked his elbows on the bar so he could study the room without appearing to be looking at anyone in particular. The woman in question sat with her back to the wall, talking with one of the saloon's other 'soiled doves.' Even from where he stood, Orrin could tell one side of her face was swollen, the eye surrounded by deep purplish bruising. The process of healing left the bruise with shades of yellow and green around the edges. 'Quite a shiner,' he observed.

'Her name's Doris. She's the third one of my girls he's beat up. Always says he's sorry, an' promises it won't happen again. Then he treats 'em like human beings again for a while, 'cause I tell 'im I don't want his business if he don't. He done that to Doris about a week an' a half ago.'

Orrin mulled over the information while he nursed another sip of the whiskey. 'Well, I gotta hang around a few days anyway,' he said, more to himself than to the bartender. 'Might just as well make good use of the time.'

3

There is a rule in the high country of Wyoming that is inviolate. It is especially so for those living alone. It is this: When you step outside, you do so dressed to stay outside indefinitely.

You may be only making a quick trip to the outhouse. You may only be checking to be sure you shut the corral gate. You may be hurrying because the dog's barking indicates the presence of some varmint that you may miss the chance to shoot if you stop to put on boots, coat, gloves.

Just making a quick trip outside, it's almost never that anything unexpected happens.

'Almost never,' has a nasty ring of frequency.

Howard Dubray, or Harold Danson, or Harlan Dubolt, or whatever name to which he laid claim at the moment, well knew the rule. Like all rules in his life, however, it was made to be broken.

The cabin he had built sat in the timber along the upper reaches of Beaver Creek. The broad valley there was verdant with deep grass in even the driest of years. The ponds made by the creek's namesake rodents were frozen solid now, but they made the valley a wetlands heaven in summer.

Most people of that country would have chosen the site for its potential for raising either cattle or horses. Howard had chosen it for its isolation and near inaccessibility in winter. Even aside from his nefarious means of making a living, he just plain hated people. He wanted to be as far away from them as possible.

When he did venture into civilization it was usually to procure supplies, get drunk, and spend a bit of time with whatever 'doves of the roost,' as he called them were available. His other reason to leave his cabin was to make an occasional foray into the surrounding area wherever he and his friend could find a lucrative target to rob. Once they had made their getaway, he could retreat to his lonely hideaway with little fear.

Accordingly, he had built a tight, snug cabin, a corral and horse shelter, dug a well, and even put in a root cellar just behind the cabin. He cut enough hay in the summer to make a huge haystack against the back side of the corral. It not only provided additional windbreak for his animals, but feed for them through the heart of winter as well. He only went to town about once a month in good weather. He really didn't need to go to town at all when the weather was bad.

The winter wind had swept down from the mountain peaks the day before, bringing yet another plunge in the already frigid temperatures. A foot and a half of snow had fallen, piling in deep drifts behind everything that broke the sweep of the wind. It showed no signs of abating. Wherever the wind could reach unhindered, the frozen ground was scoured almost clear.

Around the cabin on three sides, there was an almost three foot area that the wind had blown bare. At the edge of that wind-cleared circle, the snow piled up in a smooth concave. The top of the drift reached back toward the cabin almost far enough to touch the eave.

On the other side of the cabin, its windbreak had found itself insufficient to maintain that narrow cleared area. The snow on that side was drifted deep enough to completely obliterate all view of the cabin. If seen from that direction, it would appear only as a huge, unbroken, white drift.

Storm or no storm, Dubray had to do two things. He had to make his way to the shed at the back of the corral to get water and feed to the horses, huddled there against the freezing wind. He also had to get water for himself.

The pump was at the corner of the

corral. It would take less than five minutes to pump water to fill the two buckets. Another ten minutes should be plenty of time to carry them into the shed and dump them in the trough. There was no purpose to be served by taking them more than two buckets. That was more than adequate for the three horses. What they didn't drink right away would be frozen solid within the hour.

Those with no experience with livestock in winter believe animals can subsist on the moisture in snow during cold weather. The truth is, they cannot. During severe storms, cut off from whatever source of open water that is otherwise available, more livestock perish from thirst than from the cold. They freeze to death, because they first begin to dehydrate.

The same is also true of people, so Dubray was forced to get water to the horses, then take a bucket of it into the cabin for himself. Even allowing for time to throw a couple pitchforks of hay over the corral fence into the shed, he'd be outside for no more than fifteen or twenty minutes at most.

Dubray was slack about rules, but at the same time he wasn't stupid. He knew how cold it was outside. He knew how hard the wind was blowing. Accordingly he pulled on his heavy coat, chose a pair of heavy gloves instead of mittens, which would have been warmer. He eschewed the 'Scotch cap' with its ear flaps, that would cover not only his ears but the back of his neck as well. He was, after all, a cowboy. A cowboy might tie a large rag over the top of his hat and tie it under his chin, pulling his hat brim down to protect his ears, but it was only extreme circumstances that would force him to exchange the hat for the 'dirt farmer's cap'.

As he forced his way through the chest high snow at the edge of the drift, the full force of the wind's fury first slammed against him. It instantly jerked the hat from his head, sending it sailing into the air. It caught in the timber two hundred yards from Dubray, almost totally obscured by the swirling snow.

He swore vehemently as he watched it soar away. When it hung up in the lower limbs of a tree, he started after it, lunging his way through the deep snow. Just as he was almost to it, the swirling wind lifted it from its tentative perch. It tumbled over and over, sometimes lifting high in the air, then plummeting to the ground, only to be lifted again by the mindless vagaries of the fierce wind.

Dubray continued to pursue it, flailing his way through drift after drift, cursing vehemently. He fought his way through the deep snow until he had, once again, almost reached it. He extended a hand to grab it. As if watched by some unseen jester, the wind chose that instant to lift the hat and carry it twenty yards further, just beyond another deep snow drift.

He pondered whether to keep pursuing it. He was out of breath, puffing heavily. He stood with his hands on his knees, sucking in great gulps of the frigid air. A small voice in the back of his mind whispered a warning, that he was about to freeze the lining of his lungs by breathing that heavily. If that happened, he would die in spite of anything he or anyone else could do.

He forced himself to breathe through his nose, so his body could heat the incoming air enough to keep that from happening. The effort caused it to take longer than it otherwise would have to catch his breath and breathe normally.

He started toward his hat, nearly invisible in the thick, swirling snow. There was little shelter where it had come to rest. The snow between it and him was especially deep. Another gust of wind may well pick it up and once again carry it further just about the time he reached it.

He looked back toward the cabin door. It was no longer visible through the storm. He knew, however, that he was closer to the corral than to the cabin. He decided he could tolerate the cold long enough without the hat to get the chores done. He fought his way back to where he had dropped the buckets and picked them up.

At the pump, he sat one of the buckets beneath the spout and began raising and lowering the pump handle as rapidly as possible. In half a dozen pumps water began gushing out. Even though the water was cold, it was so much warmer than the air that it steamed as if it were boiling hot. As it did, the wisps of vapor were snatched away instantly by the fierce wind.

When the bucket was full he reached down and jerked it out from under the spout. At the same time he grabbed the other bucket with the other hand, putting it where the first bucket had been. In his haste, he slopped water all over the hand that jerked the filled bucket out of the way.

He cursed as if the water had soaked his glove deliberately. If he were going to be outside any length of time, the wet glove would be a problem. Oh well.

He didn't plan to be outside long. Already his ear and cheek on the windward side of his face was stinging sharply with its frostbite warning.

He grabbed the pump handle to fill the second bucket. The wet glove froze to the handle instantly.

He didn't realize how firmly it had done so until the bucket was filled. He released the handle and pulled his hand away. The hand slid out of the glove, leaving it clinging tightly to the iron handle.

He swore again. He grabbed the glove and jerked. It stayed where it was, resisting his effort.

The first real alarm bells began to ring in his head. It was far colder out here than he had realized.

He forced himself to be calm. He pulled at one finger of the frozen glove at a time until he worked it loose from its icy grip on the pump handle. With difficulty he got his hand back inside of it, though it was already frozen too stiff to do so easily. To pick up a bucket of water with that hand, he had to take the other hand and bend his fingers around the pail. He picked up the other bucket with his free hand, and forced his way through the snow toward the horses.

Stepping into the shelter of the shed was an instant, almost overwhelming relief. The break from the wind and the animal heat given off by the horses made it almost bearable in the tight circle close to them. He dumped the water into the trough. All three horses had their noses in the water, slurping eagerly, before he had finished filling the trough. Setting the buckets out of the way of the horses, he climbed through the rails of the corral. He quickly threw three pitchforks of hay over the fence, aiming it around the corner of the shed so it would land inside, where they stood out of the wind.

He jammed the pitchfork back into the haystack, climbed back through, and picked up the buckets. Fifteen feet later he was back in the full force of the wind. He could no longer feel either of his ears. That was a pleasant relief from the severe stinging and burning that had been warning him of imminent frostbite, but he took no pleasure in it. He well knew the intense pain he would experience as they warmed up, once he was back in the cabin.

He stopped at the pump long enough to fill one of the buckets. Carrying it and the empty one, he lunged his way through the snow, back toward the cabin. The heavily falling snow and high wind had totally obliterated all trace of the passage he had made out to the corral just a few minutes before. The hand in the wet glove was numb. His face felt stiff, as if it would crack and break if he moved it.

Shoving his way through the snow, he reached the area the wind had cleared around the near side of the cabin. Because it had drifted back just as high as it had been before, he had to lunge extra hard to break through that last barrier into the open ground. As he broke clear, he lost his balance. He fell headlong. Instinctively, he flung his hands forward in a vain attempt to break his fall. The bucket of water remained gripped in the hand with the frozen glove. It had the effect of dumping the contents directly on to him, dousing his upper body, soaking him to the skin.

It has been said that profanity is the last resort of a non-achiever, of a failure. If so, that last resort turned the already frigid air blue.

He struggled to his feet. He grabbed the bucket and looked at it, trying to think clearly. There were a couple cups of water left in the bucket at most. He walked back to the edge of the giant drift and whipped the bucket through the soft snow, filling it instantly with the light powder. It would melt down to a quart of water at most, but it would have to be enough for now.

He staggered to the cabin door. He grasped the leather thong that hung through the hole in the door. The other end of the thong was fastened to the bar that dropped into the keeper to bolt the door from the inside. He tried to grip it to pull hard enough to lift the wooden bar. His hand refused to squeeze shut enough to grip it.

He set the bucket down and worked the leather thong into a position between his hands, so he could press his hands together tightly enough to pull it. Anger surged through him. He gave a mighty jerk. The leather thong snapped and came loose in his hands.

He stood in his tracks, staring at the broken piece of leather. He struggled to concentrate, to think. He was so cold. The enormity of what had just happened seeped into his sluggish mind. He was locked out! On the other side of that door was warmth, life, comfort. It might just as well have been a hundred miles away.

It occurred to him that he might be able to slip his knife blade between the door and the jamb far enough to catch the bar and lift it. He grabbed for his knife. He couldn't feel the handle where it should have been on his belt.

He pulled his coat back and looked down. The knife sheath was empty. He frowned in sluggish confusion. Slowly, he remembered leaving it lying on the table before he went out to do the chores.

He thought about the root cellar on the other side of the cabin. It would be warm down there. Its door had a large iron ring, so he could lift it straight up. Hugging his coat around himself, he walked around the cabin. At the back corner he stopped, staring as if his mind once again was incapable of processing the information his eyes provided. Snow ten or twelve feet deep covered the ground on that side of the cabin. It was beyond impossible for him to dig his way to the root cellar. Even if he tried, using only his hands, the incessant wind would drift it back in faster than he could move it away.

He hoisted his coat up so it covered his head and wrapped it as closely around himself as he could. He struggled his way back around to the front of the cabin. He leaned back against the cabin door. He fought to make his brain work, to think of what to do. He seemed to be trapped in some kind of fog that made thinking impossible. He slid down the door in slow motion until he was sitting, huddled into a ball, at the door's base.

At least it wasn't as cold here. Maybe the storm was letting up. He didn't feel as cold, anyway. Actually he didn't feel all that cold, right now. He was sleepy, though. Really sleepy. He decided he'd just huddle here out of the wind and think about what to do. Just for a few minutes.

4

It was still pitch black when Orrin lit a lantern in the livery barn. It was warm inside. The musky smell of the horses was mild enough to be pleasant. 'The hostler keeps a clean stable,' he noted silently.

Moving quietly in case the hostler had sleeping quarters in the back, he gave his horse a bait of oats and filled his water trough. While the animal ate and drank, he brushed him down good, put on the saddle and bridle, and tied his extra-large winter bedroll behind the saddle.

He was well-dressed for winter, even at this altitude. Over his woollen long-johns, he wore heavy wool trousers and a wool shirt. The ubiquitous neckerchief was wool plaid, rather than the lighter material favoured in better weather. A sheepskin lined vest was buttoned all the way up. Over it, he wore the long, heavy winter coat, with the split tail that allowed it to hang well over the saddle. In his coat pocket was a pair of fur-lined leather gloves. In the other coat pocket was a pair of heavy winter mittens that he intended to wear.

He was two miles out of Elkhorn City before the first glimmers of the still-hidden sun began to illuminate the sparkles of frost in the sky. Almost before the eastern horizon was light enough to betray the dawn, grey overcast crowded out all hope of any warming sunshine.

The air was still. Eerily still, Orrin thought. Yesterday he thought the wind would never stop. During the night when it did, he woke in the hotel room, grabbing for his gun, alarmed by the sudden silence. When he realized what had wakened him he grunted, 'Well, maybe the weather's broke. Maybe I'll have a nice sunny ride tomorrow.'

It was not to be. By mid-morning the

wind had begun to pick up again, bearing down from the northeast. With it the snow had begun as well. He stopped his horse, dismounted, and dug into his saddle-bag. From it he extracted a heavy wool plaid cap. It had a heavy bill that he could pull down to the top of his eyes. Its ear flaps were tied up over the top. He untied them as he put the cap on, pulling the flaps down around his face, tying the string beneath his chin. The back part of the ear flaps formed another flap that covered the back of his neck. When he turned up the collar of his coat, he was well protected from the cold. The relief for his ears and face was instantaneous.

He sighed at the next necessity. He crushed his hat into the saddle-bag from which he had removed the cap. Few things other than life and death could make him abuse a good hat that way, but he knew he could return it to something closely akin to its original shape later.

By noon he regretted the decision to

pursue the lead the bartender had furnished him. The wind was howling with demonic fury. The snow had increased steadily, until he could scarcely see more than a dozen yards ahead. If he turned into the wind, he could see nothing at all.

Dubray, or Danson, or Debolt, or De-Whoever, was worthy prey from several standpoints. He was a nasty piece of work, from all he knew about the man. The price on his head made it well worth his time and effort to run him to ground. If the bartender was right, he would not at all expect to be pursued this time of year. That in itself gave Orrin a bit of an edge. Sometimes the slightest edge was the difference between life and death in his profession.

By two hours past noon he was chilled through in spite of his careful preparations. He began to talk to his horse to distract himself from his discomfort. The horse responded with occasional twitches of her ears or bobbing of her head. Mostly she just slogged on forward, her head ducked as low as she could against the wind, determined to keep on until her master told her she could quit, or until she froze in her tracks.

'We oughta be less than a mile from where we're headed,' he tried to reassure himself and his mount. He hugged the timber as much as possible to stay out of the wind. At the same time, he couldn't stay in the timber, or even close enough to more than minimally avoid the wind's wrath. Wherever the wind was less, the snow piled deeper, making it almost impossible for his horse to navigate it. He was forced to endure the gale to stay where the wind had swept the ground enough to permit his passage.

His horse's ears shot forward. Instantly Orrin sat up tall in the saddle, abandoning the hunched over position that provided at least a little relief from the wind and snow. Faintly above the wind he caught the sound of a horse's whinny. His own horse answered immediately, perceptibly picking up her gait.

Orrin made no effort to restrict or guide the horse. He knew without being able to see it, that he had found Dubray's cabin. There was no other for miles in any direction, according to the bartender. He was just as sure the man would be securely ensconced within, able to hear nothing above the wind's howl, oblivious to anyone's arrival. For the first time he began to plan his own actions.

He decided the direct approach was his only option. He would simply burst through the door, gun drawn, and yell for the man to throw up his hands.

Out of place and totally inappropriate, a voice in his mind questioned, 'What if he hasn't eaten his hands?'

He snickered at his own twisted humour, then instantly chided himself. 'I must be gettin' too cold. I'm goin' nuts, tellin' myself stupid jokes,' he muttered. 'And I even laughed at it.'

He was almost at the cabin when he

caught his first glimpse of it. The wind abated slightly for half a minute. He grunted in surprise. Over the top of a large drift he saw the top of the wall and roof of the cabin, smoke streaming from the chimney.

At the same time a horse from the corral nickered again. Orrin tugged quickly on the reins to keep his horse from answering. He decided the best thing to do was to ride directly to the door. The horse could breast that drift better than he could on foot.

The noble mount telegraphed her reluctance, wanting to go to the other horses instead, but she obeyed. She lunged and plunged through the six foot deep snow, bursting into the wind-cleared area next to the cabin.

Orrin grunted in surprise yet again. Huddled on the threshold, a man sat motionless. His coat was pulled up over his head. His face was hidden. He watched him a long moment, waiting for some movement. There was none.

He slid from the saddle, debating

with himself whether to trade his right mitten for a glove. If he did so, he could draw his gun, even slowly, if he needed to do so. If he chose not to make the switch, he'd have to shuck the mitten as he reached for his gun.

The man seemed oblivious to his presence. His mittened hand poised above his gun butt, with the fingers of the other hand gripping the end of the mitten to pull it off if need be, he walked over and kicked the motionless man's foot. He stirred slightly and muttered something unintelligible.

'Hey! Wake up!' Orrin ordered, realizing for the first time that he was, at least, alive.

The man barely lifted his head. He again mumbled something Orrin couldn't make out.

'What happened?' Orrin demanded. 'How come you're out here?'

The man finally lifted his head, slowly realizing someone was there. 'Huh?'

'How come you're out here in the cold?'

'Huh? Oh. Can't get in,' he slurred.

'Why can't you?'

'Busted it,' he mumbled. His chin drooped back down to his chest.

Orrin looked at the door. The empty hole through which the thong should have hung told the story. He looked at the thick, heavy door. He thought for a moment, then pulled his coat back and drew the large knife from its sheath on his left hip. He stepped up beside the inert man, heedless of him now, knowing he was incapable of doing anything.

With the sharp edge downward, he worked the knife blade between the door and jamb, then started tipping it up and down, working it upward. He felt it contact the bar that held the door fast. He kept working the knife, lifting as hard as he could. 'If I bust my knife blade we'll both freeze to death,' he muttered.

It took almost ten minutes of pushing, pulling and lifting. Abruptly the bar lifted free from its keeper. The door swung open.

Relief flooded through Orrin. He stepped into the cabin and looked around as he replaced the knife in its sheath. He turned back and grabbed the man by the arms of his coat, just at the back of the shoulders. With a mighty heave he pulled him inside. The man curled up on the floor, seemingly unaware he was out of the storm.

'I'll take care of you in a minute, Felicity,' he promised his faithful mare. He shut the door again and barred it against the arctic blast.

He whipped his coat and mittens off. He grabbed the man on the floor and stripped the coat from him. He protested feebly, grasping at it as it fled his reach.

Orrin slapped him twice on each side of his face. 'Wake up!' he demanded. 'You gotta get to movin'.'

When the man failed to respond he turned from him. He opened the door of the stove and threw in several fresh pieces of wood and slammed the door shut again.

A coffee pot sat on the back edge of the stove. Orrin felt the side gingerly. It was hot, but not scalding. Looking around he spotted a mug on the table, beside a knife and a chunk of salt pork. He grabbed the mug, filled it with coffee, and knelt beside the barely conscious man.

He hoisted him to a sitting position, bracing him with his lower leg. 'Here. Drink,' he commanded.

He stuck the cup against the man's lower lip and tipped it, pouring the mildly hot liquid into his mouth. Most of it ran out again, but enough ran back down his throat to make him cough and choke.

Instantly Orrin repeated the procedure. This time he actually got him to swallow a little of the hot liquid. He choked and coughed again.

Dubray tried to push him away. 'Lemme alone,' he mumbled.

He forced another two swallows of

the warming liquid down him, then turned away. He pulled the man's boots and socks off. 'Feet don't look as bad as they might,' he observed. 'If I can get him warmed up some, he might not even lose any toes. They're gonna be all swelled up an' sore as boils, though. So are his hands, if I can save the fingers.'

He slapped the outside of the man's legs, beginning at the ankles, working his way all the way up the sides of his body. He alternately slapped and rubbed his arms and hands. Then he refilled the mug of coffee again, made hotter by the greater fire in the stove. He put it to his mouth. This time he took a couple good sized swallows before he choked and pushed it away.

Walking over to the table, Orrin lit the kerosene lamp. He carried it with him and walked a complete circle around the cabin. He gathered up two pistols, two rifles, and a short double-barrelled shotgun. He emptied all of them of ammunition, wrapped them in a blanket, and shoved them under the narrow bed.

Dubray began to shiver. It started slowly, with slight tremors. Then it seemed to take over his whole body. Within a minute he was shaking so hard the table in the middle of the floor began to jiggle. 'By Jing, I think he's gonna make it,' Orrin murmured.

Looking around he spotted a length of rope. He tied the man's hands together in front of him.

From a heavy piece of leather that was draped over a chair, he cut a strip just under half an inch wide, about a foot and a half long. Walking to the door he replaced the broken thong, shoving the free end out through the hole in the door. Opening the door, he tied a double knot about an inch from the end, so it couldn't be pulled back inside without opening the door and cutting it.

He surveyed his helplessly shivering captive again. Satisfied, he put his coat and mittens back on. Dubray was lying on his side, shivering as if in some sort of seizure, and moaning with pain. Taking one more look at him, Orrin went back out into the storm.

He led his horse to where the other mounts huddled in the shed. He removed the bridle and loosened the cinch, but left the saddle on, deeming it at least some cover against the cold. He retrieved the abandoned bucket and watered his own horse and the others. He forked more hay over to them than they really needed. He knew more of it would get trampled down and used as bedding than eaten. That was just fine. They'd stay warmer that way. He didn't intend on Dubray's horses needing it to get through the rest of the winter anyway.

He filled the bucket with water and took it with him to the house. Outside the door he set it down, traded his right mitten for one of the gloves in his pocket, and drew his pistol. He pulled the thong and shoved the door open with his left hand, holding his gun levelled as if expecting to be fired on.

Dubray was warming up even faster than he had anticipated. He had not only managed a return to complete consciousness, he had found where Orrin had stashed his weapons. As Orrin stepped in through the door he pulled a Russian .44 from the wad of blankets. Still shivering so hard the weapon wobbled randomly, he swung it upward. He tried to hold it with hands still bound together and barely responsive to his efforts. He managed to squeeze the trigger. The hammer fell on the empty chamber. He thumbed the hammer and tried to shoot twice more before he realized the bullets had been removed. He swore venomously.

Orrin stepped across the room and kicked the gun out of his hand. In the same motion he slammed his Colt .45 alongside Dubray's head, knocking him to the floor, unconscious.

'I figured he'd be just about that grateful to me for savin' his life,' Orrin muttered. 'I shoulda just let 'im freeze to death, then just hauled his dead body to town.'

It would have been far less trouble.

5

Their eyes met for the barest instant. It should have gone all but unnoticed by either. It didn't.

He was riding slowly down the street, watchful as always. There were not too many folks out and about. The weather had moderated dramatically, but it was far from shirt-sleeve weather. The frozen earth was still weeks away from feeling the first loosening of winter's icy grip that held it. The sun shone bravely, but it fought in vain to lift the temperature more than a few degrees.

Part of being a bounty hunter was being always on high alert. Habitually he scanned the faces of anyone on the street. If something set off a subconscious alarm in his mind, his eyes would dart back to whatever or whomever it was.

For completely different reasons, kids

were always worthy of a second look. They were just fun to watch. Their energy level, their excitable nature, their enthusiasm for life was both a wonder to him and a source of encouragement. It served as an antidote to the steady diet of outlaws and killers and ne'er-do-wells his lot fell to pursuing.

That one electric instant may have been so striking because he wasn't expecting it. His eyes were just idly scanning, maintaining the habit of his survival. Then their eyes met. It felt as if some sudden shock went through him. His eyes widened. His head snapped around to look again. In the same instant he noted the same reaction in her. Their eyes met a second time with the same effect.

She quickly looked the other way. She began to walk faster. A hundred feet further along the board sidewalk, she stole another glance over her shoulder.

As their eyes met that second time, Orrin jerked the reins of his horse, bringing him to an abrupt halt. He hadn't even realized he had done so. He watched the young woman as if she had captured his attention with a grip he couldn't resist. He was still watching when she stole that furtive glance over her shoulder. He didn't understand why she was suddenly in such a hurry. He certainly didn't understand what was going on with himself.

His heart raced as if he had just sprinted a quarter mile. His chest felt heavy, as if he needed to draw a deep breath and couldn't do so. His mouth hung open.

A moment later his hand lifted to his face. He felt the coarseness of his beard. He knew his hair flared out in unkempt tangles from beneath the tall Stetson, still less than pristine from its time crushed into his saddle-bag. His eyes jerked up the street to where a barber's pole indicated the availability of his much-needed tonsorial grooming.

Creaking saddle leather on the other

side of him jerked his attention back to the business at hand. He silently cursed himself for the distraction he had allowed that meeting of eyes to incur. He eyed his prisoner, assuring himself the man was still securely restrained.

On his left, about six feet behind him, Howard Dubray glared in helpless rage. He was dressed warmly enough, but still shivered constantly. The wool plaid Scotch cap pulled clear down to his eyes, with its ear flaps tied under his chin, belied his reputation as a tough and dangerous man. He would rather have frozen his ears completely off than be paraded down the street in what he considered a 'back-east-dirt-farmer's-cap'.

His humiliation was furthered by the fact that his hands were trussed to the saddle horn. They were swollen and excruciatingly painful from frostbite. Even inside the heavy mittens the cold felt like fire against them. His feet were tied together beneath the horse's torso. There were no reins. Instead of a bridle, the horse had only a halter. One end of a rope led from the halter ring to Orrin's saddle horn.

Behind the captive outlaw, two extra horses trailed single file. They were tethered horse to horse, the lariat secured to each's halter.

Stopping in front of the marshal's office, Orrin stepped from the saddle. He tied the lead rope securely to the hitchrail, but simply draped the reins of his own horse across it, confident the mare would need no further hindrance from wandering.

He ran his eyes across the ropes securing his prisoner, making sure the man would remain as he was. He stepped across the board sidewalk and opened the door. Marshal Clive Missner grunted as he recognized Orrin. He leaned to the side and spat a brown stream at the cuspidor beside his desk.

'Now what?' he demanded.

'Thought I'd bring you a boarder.'

'A boarder? Do I look like I run a boardin' house?'

Orrin grinned. He jutted his chin toward the three cells at the rear of the marshal's office. 'Not a very fancy one, but it seems to have beds.'

Instead of answering, the marshal stared, waiting for some explanation. Orrin pulled the same wrinkled wanted poster from his inside pocket he had shown to the bartender. He paused to glance out the small window, checking on his prisoner, then handed it to the marshal. 'I managed to bring this one in alive.'

Missner grunted again as he looked at the picture on the poster. 'I know 'im. Surly sort of a guy. That ain't the name he's known by around here, though.'

Orrin shrugged. 'I know three or four names he's gone by. I doubt if any of 'em is his real name. Anyway, he's out front.'

'How'd you chase him down?'

'Found out where he had a cabin. Rode out there the day o' the last storm.'

'I heard you rode out that mornin'. I figgered someone'd find you, come spring, when the snow bank melted that you was froze under.'

'It did turn plumb cold.'

'I'm surprised you got Danson, or Dubray, or whatever his name is, without havin' to shoot 'im.'

Orrin glanced out the window at his prisoner again. 'Actually, I guess I sorta saved his life. He'd got himself locked outa've his cabin, soakin' wet with no hat. He was too cold to be really conscious. I managed to get the door open and get him inside and warmed up, without his even losin' any fingers or toes. One ear ain't gonna be the same, even if it don't fall off.'

'Is that so? Saved his life by goin' out there after 'im, huh?'

'Yeah.'

'So figgerin' he'll get hung, did you save 'is life or take it? Does it count with the Almighty, you reckon, if you save a man's life so's he can die by hangin'? Does He give you credit for

59

savin' one, or charge a sin agin' ya for gettin' him killed?'

'I don't know how to think about that. I could've just left 'im sittin' there leanin' against his cabin, then hauled 'im in froze stiff across his horse. That would've been easier. I just couldn't do that. It ain't my place to take anyone's life if I don't have to. If the law hangs 'im, well an' good. I 'spect he deserves that. But I ain't got a right to take it on myself to execute anyone.'

'You'd have saved the gov'ment some money, if you had. Now he'll have to be took all the way back to Nebrasky, where they put up the reward.'

'Yeah. It would've saved me a lot o' trouble too. He's tried to kill me three times since I saved his life. He mighta got the job done once, if his hands weren't so swelled up an' sore.'

'Maybe he don't think haulin' 'im in to get hung classifies as savin' his life.'

'Yeah, well, maybe it don't. But if you'll give me a hand gettin' 'im in here, he'll be your worry, an' I won't have to think about that.'

Missner heaved himself out of his chair. 'Well, the missus'll be happy. The town pays her for feedin' prisoners. Ain't had anyone in the jug more'n a couple days at a time all winter.'

They walked outside together. Dubray swore at them as soon as they did. 'About time you got around to comin' out after me,' he complained, labelling both of them with a couple choice names. 'I thought you was gonna leave me sit here till I froze to death.'

Orrin and Missner exchanged looks. As if inspired by the same thought, they both wheeled and walked back into the marshal's office, closing the door against all the names Dubray hurled at them when he realized what they were doing.

'He seems a little hot under the collar,' Missner observed as he settled back in his chair.

'You'd think he'd have chilled out a little ridin' that far, wouldn't you?'

Orrin responded, settling into the other chair.

'Maybe it's the cap.'

'You suppose that's what's got 'im riled up? He must like it. It's his cap. His hat blew off, he said. Seemed only right to put somethin' on his head for the ride into town. I sure wouldn't put a cap o' mine on his head. I suppose I could've just tied something around his head and tied it under his chin, like a woman's headscarf.'

Missner chuckled at the thought. 'He didn't have nothin' with a nice bright coloured fringe around it?'

Dubray was streaming curses loudly enough to hear him well, even though the door was shut. Both men studiously ignored him.

'Didn't notice anything like that. You'd have thought that good Scotch cap was just as bad, though, the way he cussed me out for puttin' it on 'im.'

'What did he expect you to do?'

'Go find his hat that blew away.'

Missner snorted. 'He actually thought

you could find it? Or that you'd go lookin' for it?'

'He was hopin'. I'm sure he'd have had a surprise o' some sort cooked up for me by the time I got back, if I was dumb enough to go chasin' after it.'

'Maybe since he don't like that cap, he'd cool off out there faster if we went an' took it off of him. Leave him bareheaded out there for a while, and he might get easier to listen to.'

'I doubt it. He's been cussin' a blue streak since he thawed out enough to talk. A time or two I pert neart stuffed one of his socks in his mouth.'

'If he talks like that in front o' the missus when she brings his food, that's exactly what's gonna happen, I'll tell you that.'

They sat and chatted about nothing in general for a full hour. Halfway through that hour, Dubray finally realized he was going to be left shivering there until he shut up. His teeth were chattering loudly when they finally untied him and brought him inside to a waiting cell.

When he was safely ensconced, the marshal said, 'I'll send off the wire and get your money for this one a-comin'. They'll let me know when an' how they want 'im hauled back there for trial. Oh, by the way, your money for the one you shot is waitin' for you at Western Union.'

Orrin nodded with satisfaction. 'Thanks. Now you're gonna have to put up with me hangin' around town even longer, though, waitin' for this one to come through.'

Missner gave him a long look. Finally he said, 'I didn't ever think I'd say this to a bounty hunter, but I don't have a problem with you stayin' around town as long as you like. We got an uncommon number of hard cases stoppin' into town on a sorta reg'lar basis. I might could use a bit o' back-up once in a while, as long as you're coolin' your heels around anyway.'

'Why would you have a lot of 'em here?'

The marshal studied him a long moment. 'Foster's Hole.'

'I've heard of it. Never knew where it was, till the bartender mentioned it. It's around here close?'

'It's up the river a-ways. Right nice valley, to tell the truth. Or it used to be. Then someone figgered out it'd make a plumb good natural fort. The river runs into it from the top end through a gulch too steep an' high to get through. The cliffs run up right from the water's edge. From the bottom end there's a good trail, but two men up in the rocks could stand off an army if they had to. So it just naturally come to be a spot where hard cases could hole up.'

'Sorta like the Hole-In-The-Wall, huh?'

'Yup, but even better. Nice broad valley once you're in it. Some o' them guys even got their families livin' up there. They figger the law can't touch 'em.'

'Not good news for the town, here.'

'That's a fact. One o' these times

we'll most likely have to talk the gov'nor inta sendin' in the army. It'd take cannons to knock them sentries outa the rocks.'

'Sounds like you got your hands full.'

'That's true for a fact. That's why I said I wouldn't mind havin' you hang around.'

Surprised, Orrin watched the marshal a long moment, waiting for the punch line to some dry joke the man was setting him up for. When it became evident his comment was sincere, he said, 'Thanks. I didn't expect that.'

6

'Father, did you see that man with the prisoner come into town?'

'Uh huh. Mighty fine lookin' mare he was ridin'. Fifteen hands, easy.'

'Do you know who he is?'

Brittle Eisenbraugh, who disdained to use his first name, preferring simply, 'Brit,' glanced at his wife, then over his shoulder at his daughter. 'Not really. Why?'

'Just curious,' she evaded.

'He is as rough-looking as any man I've seen in a long time,' Leah Eisenbraugh offered. 'Well, except some of those men from Foster's Hole. Some of them look more like animals than men.'

'This man didn't,' Lora Lee countered. 'Do you know who his prisoner was?'

'Fella named Danson, I heard,' Brit

related. 'Wanted for murder back in Nebraska it seems.'

'So the other man is a lawman of some kind?' Lora Lee pressed.

'Why the interest in him?' Brit demanded.

Silence betrayed the conversation was something other than casual. After a long moment Lora Lee said, 'I don't know, really. I just saw him as he was riding in with the prisoner. Something about him just caught my eye.'

'Something about him made me shudder,' Leah argued.

'His eyes didn't look like those men from Foster's Hole,' Lora Lee argued. 'They all look like . . . oh, I don't know. There's something in their eyes that scares me. Like looking at the eyes of a mountain lion. That always makes chills run down my back. But this man didn't have that look.'

'When were you close to him long enough to figure all that out?'

'I wasn't, really,' Lora Lee protested instantly. 'I only just saw him that once.

He turned and looked back at me twice.'

'You openly stared at a stranger on the street long enough for him to look back twice?' Leah accused.

Lora Lee was happy her muffler covered her face enough so her parents couldn't see her cheeks redden. 'It wasn't like that, Mother,' she protested again. 'Our eyes just met once. Then when I looked back at him, he was still looking at me. Then I looked over my shoulder again and he was looking at me again.'

'He's a bounty hunter,' Leah said. Her emphasis gave the words the same effect that 'pariah,' or 'leper,' would carry. 'He kills people for money.'

'Then why did he bring . . . Danson? Is that what you said, Father? Why did he bring him in alive? That must have been awfully difficult to do, in the awful weather we've been having.'

Neither parent offered an immediate answer. Finally Brit glanced at his wife, then said, 'I ain't all that sure that all bounty hunters is bad. It don't seem to me there's a whole lotta difference between that an' a marshal or a sheriff or somebody trackin' down an outlaw an' either bringin' him in as a prisoner or killin' him a-tryin'.'

'They wear a badge,' Leah insisted. 'That makes all the difference.'

'Well, the word around town is that Missner might just make this guy a deputy town marshal, to help 'im deal with them guys that drift in from time to time from Foster's Hole.'

'Then he'd be wearing a badge, too,' Lora Lee injected.

'The town council would never approve that,' Leah insisted.

'They wouldn't have to, if he don't pay 'im wages,' Brit suggested.

'He can't just deputize somebody on his own.'

'I don't know. I think he can. If he hired him on for wages, the town council would have to approve the pay. But if he ain't spendin' any o' the town's money, I don't know as they would.'

'Don't bounty hunters just go after really bad people?' Lora Lee insisted.

'They do it for money,' Leah repeated her earlier argument. 'That makes it blood money.'

'So is it blood money if Marshal Missner shoots the same man? He gets paid money for it,' Lora Lee shot back.

'Bounty hunters are gunfighters.'

'So is Marshal Missner if he shoots somebody with a gun.'

'Stop trying to argue with everything I say, young lady. There's a difference, and you know it.'

'Oh. Like the difference between you and father running off to get married, and Martha Corbett running off to marry that cowboy that worked for her father?' Lora Lee defied.

'How come you're so all-fired anxious to defend this bounty hunter?' Brit demanded, trying to fend off the brewing battle between the two women in his life.

'I'm not defending him,' Lora Lee protested. 'I only saw him that once. I just don't think it's fair to paint all bounty hunters with the same brush. There have to be good ones and bad ones.'

'Oh, and you can tell the good ones, just by looking into their eyes,' Leah persisted.

Brit scrunched down further on the seat of the buckboard, more from discomfort with his wife and daughter bickering than from the cold. 'Let's just change the subject,' he requested.

They didn't really change the subject. They just lapsed into silence until they drove into the yard of the L-Bar-E Ranch.

Brit stopped the conveyance in front of the main house. He helped his wife, then his daughter step down. By the time they did, three hands had come out of the bunkhouse. The cowboys carried the goods Leah directed into the house. Then one of them climbed into the seat and drove the buckboard to the cook house to unload the supplies there, then to the barn for what belonged there.

Brit could have simply gone on into the house, knowing his hands would take good and proper care of everything. But if he took care of the horses himself, he wouldn't find himself in the middle of another argument between Leah and Lora Lee. Being a man of wisdom, he opted for the horses.

7

'Padlock 'im to the ring, Earl.'

The man designated 'Earl,' moved around Dubray, careful to avoid placing himself between the outlaw and the double barrelled shotgun the US marshal held levelled and ready.

'Slide back a-ways,' Earl ordered.

Dubray loosed another salvo of vulgar descriptions of both lawmen, but didn't move. Earl reached out and grabbed him by an ear lobe. Dubray howled with pain and outrage as he pulled. 'Lay off! My ears are still sore as boils!' he yelled.

'Then slide back where I can fasten the chain to the ring,' Earl commanded.

Continuing to berate the patient lawman with every profanity he knew, he complied. Earl slid the padlock through the ring, then through a link of the chain that bound Dubray, then snapped it shut.

'You ain't gonna haul me all the way to Nebrasky like this, are you?' he protested.

'If you behave we will,' the marshal confirmed. 'If you don't, we'll toss you off the tailgate and drag you.'

His comment was met with another barrage of profanity. Wordlessly, the marshal reversed his grip on the shotgun and slammed the butt of it into the outlaw's mouth. Blood flew in all directions. 'Either you harness that tongue o' yours, or you ain't gonna have any teeth left by the time we get there,' the marshal advised in a voice as calm as if he were discussing a saddle.

Orrin smiled tightly. 'He don't seem any more disposed to listen to all that than you did,' he observed to Clive Missner, standing beside him.

Missner shrugged. 'No need to knock his teeth out, though. All I had to do was handcuff 'im, stuff one of his socks in his mouth, then tie it there with his neckerchief. One whole day thataway, and he was plumb willin' to keep a civil tongue in his head. Especially when the wife was there, bringin' his eats.'

'If he'd have washed them socks this year, it wouldn't have been so bad.'

'Wouldn't have worked so good, neither.'

Orrin chuckled. He fingered the badge pinned to his vest. It felt good to wear a badge, even if it carried with it no real authority outside of town. The money for his capture of Dubray had come through. With the money he had stashed in banks in other places, he had a substantial grubstake.

He felt especially good watching someone else take the outlaw off their hands. He had dreaded the task he knew Marshal Missner was going to assign him. Transporting Dubray all the way to Nebraska would be far more trouble than the extra pay he would receive for doing so would offset. He was relieved when Missner received a wire that a United States Marshal and his deputy would be arriving to carry out that duty.

The US marshal explained it was necessary, crossing various jurisdictions, that a federal officer be in charge. They also deemed it necessary to have at least two of them doing so, aware that the outlaw was both resourceful and deadly. One man alone would have scarce dared to sleep during the trip.

They had come prepared to put Dubray in the back of a spring wagon, shackled hand and foot, and secured to an eye-bolt fastened to the wagon's bed. It would be a long ride indeed for the outlaw, sitting flat with nothing to cushion the bumps and jars of the journey. He might be bruised and sore enough by the time they got there that being hung would be a relief.

Orrin and Clive Missner had struck up a surprising friendship. In spite of his less than meticulous personal hygiene, the marshal was enjoyable to be around. He had a dry, almost sardonic wit that Orrin found refreshing. He was totally without pretence or apology for who and what he was. You could like him, hate him, or ignore him — it made the marshal no difference.

Twice since wearing a badge he had stood with the marshal and backed down some tough characters. They had come into town, presumably from Foster's Hole, to let off steam and party. They were not interfered with until their rowdiness became threatening to local citizenry. When they were confronted, there would almost certainly have been gunplay if Orrin and Missner had not been together. They were obviously well aware of the reputations of both men, and thought better than to challenge the two of them.

Aware of the likelihood that most of the residents of Foster's Hole would be wanted somewhere, the marshal had sent out telegrams with descriptions of the ones he had seen, seeking information. While he waited for some response, Orrin spent a lot of time in the Silver Dollar. Almost never sampling the establishment's wares, he nonetheless kept their supply of black coffee fresh. Chatting with the saloon's customers, joining in an occasional card game, and doing a lot of listening, he became well acquainted with many of the townfolk. He even came to know a lot about the ones that never frequented the saloon. Gossip, after all, is always the number one attraction of small towns.

Sitting in on a poker game, holding jacks and kings, waiting for the one card he called for, was not the time to be distracted. Even so, he was.

The big man had been there nearly two hours. He had bought one of the 'crib girls' several drinks. As was normal procedure, the drinks the bartender brought her were mostly tea, but the man grew more and more vocal, more and more belligerent, as he continued to drink.

Orrin had no idea what raised the man's ire. That he and the 'horizontal worker' had a disagreement was beyond question. His language became more foul as its volume increased. Finally Orrin laid his hand down on the table and rose to quell the disturbance.

Just as he approached the table where the two sat, the man reached across the table and backhanded the woman. She flew from her chair, landing in the sawdust that covered the floor.

Without thought or intention, Orrin slammed his fist into the side of the man's head, sending him sprawling into the same sawdust.

To his surprise, the man sprang cat-like to his feet. He sent a left hook that caught Orrin on the tip of the chin, even as he was moving backward to avoid it. The man's right hand came over the top in almost the same instant, catching Orrin with enough force to stagger him backward.

Catching his balance, Orrin dodged aside from a left uppercut, and sent one of his own into the upper stomach of the woman's assailant. As the man grunted, Orrin sent a right, then a left into the same spot as rapidly as possible, then ducked away.

Three blows that hard to the man's wind should have put him out of commission. They should at least have doubled him over. Instead they seemed only to enrage him. With a growl he loosed a wild right at Orrin's head. He dodged enough to almost evade it. Even so, it connected with enough force to make lights dance in his eyes and make his left ear roar.

He ducked into a crouch just in time to miss a looping left. He stood up behind it, sending a straight right hand into the big man's chin with all the force he could muster. It nearly lifted the man from his feet. He staggered back a couple steps to catch his balance, then leaned forward to renew his attack.

Timed perfectly to catch that forward motion, Orrin's left fist smashed squarely into the man's nose. His eyes went out of focus. Orrin's right fist slammed into his left cheek bone, followed at once by a hard left to his jaw.

The man staggered backward, trying to keep his balance. Orrin stepped slightly to the side and sent his right fist into the man's left temple. He toppled sideways and sprawled on the floor. He tried once to rise, then collapsed back to the sawdust.

Orrin jerked the man's gun from its holster. He shucked the shells out of the cylinder and pocketed them. He replaced the empty gun in its holster.

He glanced up and stopped abruptly. Butch Arneson was leaning on his bar. A short double-barrelled shotgun lay loosely in his grip. Orrin grunted. 'Now you show up with that,' he complained.

'Had it all the time,' Butch grinned in response. 'I was just enjoyin' the little show you put on. Entertainment's hard to come by around here.'

'You could at least have shot one barrel up in the air to put a stop to it.'

'Nope,' Butch shook his head. 'The

last time I did that I hit one o' the stovepipes. It sent out a cloud o' soot that took me three days to clean up, not to mention smokin' up the place somethin' terrible. If I shoot it now I make sure there's a good sized body in front of it to soak up all the damage.'

Orrin returned his gaze to the table where his poker game had been in progress. Three of the men were still there. One grinned and waved a hand toward Orrin's cards, still face down on the table. 'You got your full house,' he said. 'The pot's yours.'

Orrin walked back to the table. He picked up the card he had been dealt. Sure enough, it was the third jack. 'Did you look at my hand or you got the cards marked?' he asked in mock umbrage.

Clint Jackson grinned in response. 'You just never know.'

Glancing once more at the man he had whipped, Orrin raked in the pot and stuffed it in his pocket. 'Thanks, boys,' he said. He lifted his coat from the peg on the wall as he walked out.

8

'You shoulda hauled him in, while you had the chance.'

'Who?'

'That fella you whupped up on over at the Silver Dollar.'

Orrin eyed Marshal Clive Missner, trying to determine whether he was about to learn something, or if Missner was setting him up for some sort of joke. Either of the two was likely.

That caution was strong in his attitude as he asked, 'Why?'

'Well, I s'pose I could probably give you a thousand reasons.'

Orrin studied his face a long moment. The marshal's expression gave him no clue, as the man leaned over and spat a stream of tobacco juice into the cuspidor. 'How about just one reason?'

'Just one, huh?'

'Yeah. Just one.'

'A dollar.'

'What?'

'You asked for just one reason. I gave it to you. One dollar.'

'What kind of reason is that?'

'Just what you asked for. I offered you a thousand. You said you just wanted one. I can't wait to trade horses with you some time.'

'You ain't makin' any sense.'

'You ain't makin' any dollars, neither.'

'So we're both dumb an' broke. What else is new?'

'Well, I know I ain't so dumb. I know somethin' you don't seem to. An' I ain't so broke, neither. I didn't just turn down a thousand dollars an' settle for one dollar instead.'

Things began to fall into place in Orrin's mind. He fingered the bruise on his face as he said, 'Are you tellin' me that guy I whipped has a price on his head?'

'A thousand dollars' worth.'

'Really! What for?'

'Murder. Robbery. Assault.'

'Bad guy, huh?'

'Plumb bad. His was the only one o' the inquiries I sent out that got an answer that came back with a warnin'. Several of 'em is wanted, but that's the only one anyone saw fit to warn me about.'

'You got a warning?'

'Yup. Sheriff o' Lake County, down in Colorado, said he killed six people there. Five men and one woman. Shot one of 'em in cold blood. Nobody seems to know why. Beat the rest of 'em to death.'

'What with?'

'His fists. Around Leadville, the sheriff said he's the prime suspect in half a dozen robberies, too. In them he'd just up an' cold-cock someone an' then rob 'em afore they woke up. If he's mad, though, he don't stop poundin' on 'em till they're deader'n a door nail.'

'What's his name?'

'He went by Nate Niedermeyer down

there. Hard to tell what he goes by now.'

'A thousand dollars! That's a lot o' money.'

'Yeah, but if you happen to get 'im, remember I get all but one dollar of it.'

Orrin grinned. 'Sounds fair. Of course, knowing that, if I happen to spot 'im again, I'll just let you know where he is. Then you can take care of him and just give me my one dollar.'

Instead of pursuing the issue, Missner said, 'I ain't seen 'im around town since you laced 'im out, but his horse is still at the livery barn. You'd best keep your powder dry an' your eyes open.'

That very real danger was heavy on Orrin's mind as he left the marshal's office. He opened the door and started to walk out, then backed up half a step to look the street over more carefully before he ventured into it.

Just as he took that half step backward, splinters flew from the door jamb beside his head. He flung himself back into the marshal's office and sprawled on the floor. With a level of speed and dexterity that stunned Orrin almost as much as the gunshot, Missner sprang to the door, gun in hand. Staying low on one knee, peering in the direction from which the shot had come, he snapped off a quick shot with his .45.

Whirling back to Orrin he said, 'You OK?'

'Yeah. I just got a face full of kindlin'.'

'Well pick it out careful-like, an' save it for me. I like havin' some small kindlin' at hand to get the fire goin'.'

'This is a little too wet with blood to burn good.'

'It'll dry.'

'You're sure a sympathetic sort. What would you do if I was bad hurt?'

'Well, if you wasn't too bad hurt, I'd holler for someone to fetch the doctor.'

'Only if I wasn't too bad hurt?'

'Dang right. Doc Snodgrass is purty good on the stuff that ain't too bad. If you're shot bad, I wouldn't wanta waste the man's time with somethin' he ain't gonna be able to fix nohow.'

Sitting on the floor, satisfied he had picked out at least most of the wooden slivers, Orrin said, 'I don't suppose you managed to hit 'im.'

Missner shook his head. 'To tell the truth, the only thing I had a chance at was his foot, as he ran between a couple buildings. I didn't hear 'im yelp none, but it sounded like I hit somethin'. If you're able to walk, we'll wander over there an' take a look-see.'

'Why wouldn't I be able to walk? I just got a few slivers in my face.'

'You just never know. I had a deputy once that told me he couldn't walk when he got an ear ache. If his ear was hurtin', he'd stagger like a drunk cowboy.'

'He wasn't just stringin' you?'

'Nope. He was a good man, an' true, he was. He just didn't have no balance when he had one o' them ear aches.'

Orrin wiped the blood from the side of his face with his neckerchief, then thrust it in his pocket. 'Let's go have a look.'

Watching around carefully, they walked across the street together. Orrin stuck his head into the opening between the two buildings and jerked it back at once. Noting nothing of importance, he took another look, a little longer. Then he stepped into the opening. He walked the length of it, and checked the area behind the stores. When he turned back, Missner was squatted near the sidewalk, looking at something in his hand.

'What'cha got?' Orrin asked.

'If that man is as much of a heel as he's supposed to be, I reckon I got 'im.'

'You hit 'im?'

'I hit the heel, all right.'

He handed Orrin a small, oddly shaped piece of hard leather, smooth on two sides and ragged on the others. 'What is it?'

'I ain't rightly plumb sure, but I think it's a piece of a boot heel.'

Orrin studied it carefully. 'Could be

you're right. That's some mighty fine shooting, if it is. And the torn edges are fresh. That almost has to be what it is. What'dya know!'

'Don't act so surprised! You figgered cuz I'm old an' fat I couldn't shoot, did you?'

'I didn't have any idea you were that good,' Orrin admitted.

'There goes our boy, I'm bettin',' Missner announced, pointing.

Nearly a thousand yards beyond the edge of town, a horse and rider emerged from the cover of the timber and began to gallop away down the road.

'Had his horse all saddled an' ready. Went an' got him and took off, away from the road, while we were figuring out whether he was still waitin',' Orrin said, feeling as if he were mindlessly parroting some piece of information they both knew full well.

Missner picked up on that tone in his voice instantly. Seriously over-pronouncing all his words, he said, 'Mighty profound observation, Mr Bounty Hunter. An' I do believe he's ridin' right up there on top o' that horse, too,' he intoned, with affected dramatic tones.

'Well, then, Mr Marshal, I guess I'd better get a horse too, if I want to catch up with him,' Orrin observed, mimicking the marshal's tone and accent with a perfectly straight face.

'You might even wanta put a saddle on it,' Missner added.

'Wouldn't that just add more weight for my poor horse to carry?'

'Weight ain't no problem. Anyone as full o' hot air as you needs the weight to keep the horse's feet on the ground.'

'Me?! I ain't the one that started this horse opera conversation.'

'You seem to be the best one at it, though.'

Instead of answering, Orrin used his already bloody neckerchief to wipe away the blood that persisted in oozing from half a dozen spots on the side of his face. Half an hour later he was in the saddle, determined to follow the trail of the man who had tried to murder him.

9

The trail was not at all difficult to follow.

'Headin' straight for Foster's Hole,' Orrin fumed. 'Then he can bide his time and drift out whenever he feels like it and bushwhack me. Well, at least I'll learn the shortest way to Foster's Hole.'

He rode at a fast lope for the first three miles. When the bushwhacker's tracks turned off the main trail, he slowed to a trot. Tracks indicated the man he chased had done the same.

He fought the clamouring of his mind to run his horse, catch the scoundrel where he had a chance to face him one on one. He knew it would be more than foolish to do so. For two miles he allowed the horse to pick his way at a slow trot.

He kept studying the tracks. The

outlaw was making almost as good a time as he was. At this rate he would never catch up with him in time. He urged the horse to a faster gait. He should ride more slowly and carefully. He needed to make up time, to catch the outlaw before he made it into his safety zone.

The snow was gone from the south slopes of the hills. The wind had blown much of it clear, or left it with only a moderate depth of snow. The spring sun at this altitude had a lot of power. The exposed southern slopes thawed quickly. Already a hint of green grass was beginning to show in places.

Seeing bare ground tended to make a man — or a horse — grow careless. All the shaded surfaces were still frozen solid. Patches of ice were particularly treacherous when the ice on the surface began to melt. One careless step could pile horse and rider in a heap of twisted ligaments or broken bones.

It was not uncommon for a cow or horse to slip and fall in such a low spot, and never get up. The extremely slick surface, and the upward slope of the ground in all directions, made it impossible for the animal to regain its feet. It was forced to lie there until it froze, or a cowboy came along and roped it and dragged it to a place that allowed it to regain its feet, or a predator of one kind or another took advantage of an easy meal.

Against his better judgment, Orrin had been riding at a swift trot for nearly three hours. He could tell he was gaining fast on his quarry. They were still several miles from the entrance to Foster's Hole, from all he had learned of the place. Niedermeyer couldn't be more than half a mile ahead.

Pausing at the edge of a neck of timber near the crest of a rise, he caught his first glimpse of the outlaw. He was just passing out of sight over a low saddle between two ridges. He didn't bother to look back. He was riding at an almost leisurely pace, confident he would not be pursued.

Orrin touched his spurs to the mare. She responded as if she understood her master's urgency. She covered a quarter of a mile at a swift lope, then slowed to a quick trot when the ground underfoot became slick and frozen.

Orrin almost spurred her again, then refrained. If the mare slowed, it was because her instinct dictated it for safety. He took a deep breath, trying to be patient. Just then she went down.

Orrin felt one hoof slide out from under her. He jerked his leg up in time to keep it from being caught under her as she fell. He rolled clear, his gun in his hand, not at all sure whether the horse had just fallen or had been shot.

The mare struggled back to her feet, seeming none the worse for the fall. He holstered his gun. He led her away from the patch of snow and ice that had triggered her spill. As he did she limped heavily on one front leg.

He bent over and ran his hands down her leg. Just at the hock he felt her flinch. The leg was beginning to swell already.

He stood up and looked where the outlaw had disappeared over the ridge. All hope of catching up with him was gone like a wisp of smoke in the breeze.

Even as the metaphor occurred to him, he glanced over his left shoulder and saw a thin column of smoke appear for a moment, before it was snatched away by the wind. He watched the spot for a long moment before he saw it again. When the wind died down for several minutes, it made a slender finial reaching into the sky. 'There's a place over there, Felicity,' he informed the horse. 'Couple miles away, it looks like.'

Even though it was only a couple miles, it was over an hour before they walked into the ranch yard. The horse was limping badly from her injury. He was limping just as badly from having walked two miles in those riding boots.

10

The dogs' barking was stopped by a harsh word from the porch of the house. 'Quiet down out there! I seen 'im.'

Hobbling as if he were on his last legs, Orrin straightened his back. Ignoring his misery as best he could, he lengthened his stride. Fierce, fiery pain shot along the soles of his feet, up the back of his legs, burned like hot steel in his knees and sent cramps up the front of his thighs. Cowboy boots were wonderfully designed for riding. Their narrow, pointed toe made it far easier to catch the stirrup in a hurry. The tall, underslung heel — two inches farther forward at the bottom than where it attached to the boot — worked admirably to keep the foot from slipping through the stirrup when a cowboy got dumped off his horse. That design had saved innumerable lives. For walking, however, it would be hard to conceive a more effective device of torture.

Giving his best effort at manly disdain of the severe pain, Orrin walked to the porch of the house. The rancher looked vaguely familiar, but he couldn't place him.

'Looks like your horse came up lame,' he commented.

'She fell on the ice,' Orrin responded. 'At least nothin's busted, as far as I can tell.'

'I 'spect your right,' the rancher agreed. 'She wouldn't be puttin' that much weight on it if it was. Plenty sore, though. On the other hand, she don't look much lamer'n you do, from here.'

Orrin offered a rueful grin. 'These boots sure ain't made for walkin'.'

'How far'd you hafta walk?'

'Couple miles.'

'That's a-plenty. You're the bounty hunter, ain't ya?'

Orrin nodded, watching the rancher

closely to see whether that was a curse or just an observation. He saw nothing hostile. 'I was chasin' after a guy named Nate Niedermeyer. He took a pot-shot at me in town.'

'That's the fella you worked over at the saloon, ain't it?'

'That's him.'

'Well, I 'spect he's up in The Hole by now.'

'Yeah. I think I'd have caught up with him before he got to the pass if my horse didn't fall down.'

'The footin's plumb tricky this time o' year all right. Well, get down an' come in,' he offered, mouthing the inevitable invitation, even though Orrin was already off his horse. 'Put your horse up in the barn, yonder, afore ya come in. I 'spect there's a bottle or two o' liniment out there you might use on that fetlock. I ain't right sure where, but I'm sure there's some in the barn there somewhere.'

'I can show him where it is, Father.'

Orrin scarcely heard the last half

of the rancher's statement. Midway through it, the young woman stepped out beside him that Orrin had seen in town. He instantly understood why the rancher seemed vaguely familiar. Her eyes now had the same effect on him they had in that instance. That same electric shock ran through him. Everything else faded to some distant place. The rancher's words became scarcely-heard background noise, behind the suspended silence of a world unseen.

She seemed to be having an equally difficult time tearing her eyes away from his. Some part of Orrin's awareness took in the rest of her. She wasn't particularly beautiful, but she wasn't hard on the eyes, either. Her dark hair fell in natural ringlets, framing a face that was slightly large-featured. Above her full lips, her slightly aquiline nose was a bit long, but rather than distracting it lent an air of strength to her face. She was quite broad-shouldered for a woman, with arms that matched. He guessed her to be surprisingly strong. Her hips were full but not broad, again adding to that perception of strength, rather than making her look stodgy or heavy.

But it was the eyes he couldn't stop looking at. He didn't understand why. They were not that remarkable he decided, except for their effect on him. He felt as if he could almost see behind them, and sense there a depth of age-old wonders that called out silently and irresistibly to him, with a promise of world-old things.

'That ain't really necessary, ma'am,' he said, instead of vocalizing the 'Yes! Yes!' that his inner self was demanding he say. 'You don't need to trouble yourself.'

Her broad smile drove away all awareness of the intense pain in his feet and legs. 'It's no trouble,' she said. 'But my name's Lora Lee. 'Ma'am' is my mother.'

'As soon's you get that done, come on in the house,' the rancher intruded. 'Supper's pert neart ready. Oh, by the way, my name's Brit. Brit Eisenbraugh.'

Belatedly Orrin reached out a hand and returned the rancher's grip. 'Orrin Reed. Pleased to meet you. I was tryin' to guess your name on the way in, from the brand on your stock. I thought it probably started with an 'L'. Ain't your brand the L-Bar-E?'

'Yeah, I can see where that'd be a bit confusin'. Used my wife Leah's initials. A 'B' blots too bad when you try to brand.'

'That makes sense. I sure do appreciate the invite. What don't seem far a-horseback sure is a long way afoot.'

Brit simply nodded and turned back into the house. Lora Lee stepped down off the porch and headed for the barn, obviously intending for Orrin to accompany her. A team of Belgians couldn't have kept him from doing so, just then.

They exchanged easy small talk as he removed the saddle and bridle from his mare. Lora Lee poured a measure of grain into the grain box at one end of the manger. Then she climbed the ladder and dropped a pitchfork of hay into the manger as well. She was back down the ladder and pumping a bucket of water to set into a corner of the stall by the time he had finished rubbing the mare down.

She handed him a bottle of horse liniment. He knelt beside his horse and gently began rubbing the pungent liquid into the animal's lower leg. She cringed from his touch at first, then returned to munching the oats as the soothing warmth of the lotion began to ease her discomfort.

'What's her name?' Lora Lee asked.

'Felicity.'

'Really?'

'Yeah. What's wrong with that?'

'I've never heard of a man naming his horse Felicity. Trusty, maybe, but not Felicity.'

'She's a mare. Seems like she oughta have a sorta feminine name. Besides, half the horses in the country are named Trusty. Or Browny. Or Whitey.'

'Or Jack,' she grinned. 'If a cowboy doesn't have a dog named Jack he'll have at least one horse that is.'

'Yeah, either that or Shep. If you holler 'Here, Shep', real loud you'll likely have a dozen dogs come runnin'.'

She giggled. 'I had a dog once I named Deeogee.'

'Deeogee? I never heard that one.'

'Sure you have. Just say it slow.'

He frowned as he said, 'Dee-o-gee.' He barked a sudden laugh at himself as soon as the last syllable was out of his mouth. 'I bet that was just to teach your pa's cowboys how to spell it.'

She shook her head, laughing. 'It didn't work. Most of them just shortened it to Deeo without ever figuring it out.'

'Speakin' of names, I never met anyone named Brit before. I knew a Bret once, but not Brit. That from 'British'?'

'No. I'd never thought of that, but I guess it could be. It's 'Brittle'.'

'Brittle?'

'Now you know why he just goes by 'Brit'.'

'Are you two about done yackin' out here so we can eat supper?' a young voice demanded from the barn door. 'I'm hungry.'

'Who invited you out here?' Lora Lee demanded of the grinning youth.

'Ma did. She's raggin' Pa for lettin' you come out to the barn with a stranger, all by yourself.'

'That figures,' Lora Lee responded. 'Mr Reed, this is my brother, Whistle-britches.'

'My name ain't Whistle-britches!' the lad retorted. 'It's Glen. Glen Eisen-braugh. What's your name, Mister?'

'Nope,' Orrin responded with a wink at Lora Lee.

There was an instant of silence. Glen frowned. He looked from one to the other, then said, 'What?'

'I said 'Nope,' Orrin repeated.

'What's that mean?'

'It means my name ain't Mister.'

'Well I know your name ain't Mister.'

'You just asked me if it was.'

'No I didn't. I said, 'What's your name, Mister?''

'See, you just asked me again. And no, my name isn't Mister.'

'So what is your name?'

'Orrin. And I'll make you a deal.'

'What kinda deal?'

'I won't call you Whistle-britches if you don't call me Mister.'

The boy grinned. 'You got a deal . . . Orrin.'

With another covert wink in Lora Lee's direction, he said, 'We have a deal, Snizzle-biscuit.'

'What?'

'I said . . . '

'I heard what you said! Where'd the name Snizzle-biscuit come from?'

'From me. Didn't you hear me?'

'But you're supposed to call me Glen. That was the deal.'

'I didn't say I'd call you Glen. I said if you didn't call me Mister I wouldn't call you Whistle-britches. I kept our deal. Snizzle-biscuit isn't the same as

Whistle-britches at all.'

'But I don't even know what a snizzle-biscuit is.'

'That's OK. Neither do I.'

'Then why'd you call me that?'

'Because it isn't Whistle-britches.'

'But ... but ... aw, you're just funnin' me! I'm goin' in to supper.'

With that Glen whirled and left the barn, stomping the ground with each step, fists doubled at his side. Lora Lee pushed away from the edge of the horse's stall. She had been leaning against it, laughing silently at the exchange between the pair. 'We'd better get on in the house,' she suggested, a faint echo of her laughter still tingeing her voice. 'It's hard to say how that conversation is going to get reported to Mother.'

As they walked out of the barn Orrin said, 'He's a bright boy. I'm guessin' he's a lot of fun to be around.'

She nodded. 'Sometimes. Except when he doesn't know when to quit. He's so opposite from Flint.'

'Flint's your brother too?'

'Yes. You'll meet him when we get in the house. He's the one who thinks he always needs to protect me.'

'He's the one that was over in the corner of the barn?'

'Oh! You noticed him.'

'I saw him slip in just after we got there. He just stood there in the shadow. I don't think he moved a muscle the whole time.'

'Sometimes it's really irritating to have him watching over me like a mother hen. But he means well, and sometimes it's awfully nice to know he's there. Even when he doesn't think I see him. And even though he's just sixteen — well, 'almost seventeen', he keeps telling me, I think he could protect me from just about anything. Or anybody.'

'Considering some of the characters that seem to be plentiful in this part of the country, I'd think it'd be more than just nice.'

The supper Leah Eisenbraugh set on the table was almost as good as the conversation and the company. Orrin was truly glad he had arrived too late to eat supper with the crew, but before the rancher and his family had eaten. Leah was noticeably chilly in the conversation at first, but had begun to warm to him quite a bit by the end of supper.

'You ain't still gonna go after that fella, are you?' Brit asked during a lull in the conversation.

Orrin pondered the question while he chewed a bite of the roast beef that was fit for any royalty. 'Well, if I could buy or borrow a horse from you, I'd like to at least look things over. There oughta be some way to get in and out o' that valley.'

Flint looked at him strangely, as though he were finally going to contribute to the conversation, but he apparently decided against it. He turned his attention back to his supper.

Brit said, 'Well, I'll sure enough loan you a horse. I got a big gelding in the barn that I ride quite a bit. I ain't sure it'd be too smart to try to get into

Foster's Hole, though. They always got sentries watchin' the only road that goes in there.'

'There's only one?'

'So far as I know.'

Once more Orrin thought Flint was about to say something, but again he thought better of it.

'A guy can't get in from the upper end?'

'Not a chance that way, unless you got a boat that'll get through the rapids. There's a steep cliff goes up on both sides from right at the water. An' I don't think even an Indian could get a canoe through them rapids. Especially this time o' year. Even if you made it in that way, you wouldn't have no way out.'

'How many of 'em hole up in there?'

The rancher shrugged. 'Don't guess anybody knows. They come and go. There's quite a bunch, though. I'd guess twenty or more at any one time. I've heard tell some of 'em have pretty decent cabins built in there, along with a barn or two. There's at least a couple o' families, too. Once in a while a couple with two or three kids shows up in town. Gossip is they're from up there, but they never much talk to anyone. Some of 'em in there live in tents when they're there. Somebody told me once there's a regular bunk-house there, with a cook house on one end and an outhouse out behind, just like a reg'lar ranch.'

'Sounds like they pert neart got their own town in there.'

'They're as snug as a bug in a rug in there,' the rancher agreed. 'There ain't nothin' short o' the army that could ever blast 'em outa there. Sooner or later we're gonna have to do somethin', though. They're a bad bunch.'

When he did take his leave and go to the bunkhouse, he was stopped about halfway there. As if he had materialized out of the darkness, Flint suddenly stood beside him. Orrin grabbed for his gun before he recognized the lad. 'Where'd you come from?' he demanded. 'I like to jumped outa my skin.'

Instead of answering, Flint held out something to him. 'Here,' he said. 'You might need these.'

The rancher's son melted back into the night again as silently as he had appeared. Orrin stared after him, fascinated, for a long moment. Then he looked at what the boy had given him. It was a pair of moccasins. He frowned, trying to make sense of the gesture. Failing to do so, he shrugged. He decided to make a side trip to the barn and stick them in his saddle-bag. Maybe he'd figure out the reason for them later.

From the barn he made his way to the bunkhouse and stepped inside. All eyes turned to him immediately. Conversations abruptly halted, with everyone waiting silently for him to introduce himself. 'Evenin', boys. My name's Orrin Reed. Just bummin' a meal an' a bed.'

One of the hands said, 'Hey! You're the guy that beat the snot outa that big outlaw!'

Orrin nodded. 'Yeah, I guess I'm the guilty one.'

'Boy, you laid a couple o' the finest slobber-knockers on him as I ever seen anybody land. I bet his nose is too sore to touch for two weeks at least.'

That not only opened the conversation with the crew. It ensured that he was welcome among them. He learned a great deal in the course of conversation about the stress of their living and working in such close proximity to the outlaw nest.

He learned nothing that provided any idea how to get within that valley alive, much less get out again.

11

Orrin chided himself for the extra days he had spent at the L-Bar-E. Alternately he chided himself for not extending that by another day or two. Or three or four. Lora Lee's company was entirely too delightful for him to want to leave. At the same time he felt an urgency to find the man who had tried to kill him before he quit the country.

He didn't really appreciate the beauty spread before him. He didn't disdain it in any way. He was just too preoccupied to focus on it. He failed to savour the warmth with which the sun bathed him. He didn't value the verdant green swatches of land that lay alongside the dirty white drifts of old snow.

Another day, the ambience of the mountain meadow in early spring would have filled Orrin with a sense of warmth and well-being. The deep snows of a hard winter were rapidly disappearing. Green grass was visible in large patches on the south slopes, and on the flat spaces of open ground. Every small ravine ran full of snow melt.

A dozen varieties of birds sang and twittered busily from bush and tree. A meadowlark called its melodic 'oh-gee-whillikers' trill as it paused from nest building in a tall stand of last year's grass. A great eagle soared effortlessly on an updraft, watching for a mouse or a cottontail rabbit unfortunate enough to be invited to its nest for supper.

Across the broad meadow a huge bull elk lifted his head and stared at the motionless horseman. The massive rack of his antlers lifted above the tall shafts of Purple Phlox. Lower to the ground, the yellow Black-Eyed Susans, and the white Milfoil dominated, with shades of Lewis Flax and other blue and red blossoms mixed in. The explosion of stunning beauty failed to soften the frown on the bounty hunter's face.

Orrin's concentration was divided between watching for any sign of danger and seeking a course to follow. He well knew that at any time a deadly threat might erupt from the edges of the dark green timber, or from the light green of aspen groves just coming into leaf. That risk was now secondary in his mind.

The greatest challenge he faced just now was finding a way to the other side of the rushing torrent that would be a friendly and narrow creek, teeming with cutthroat and rainbow trout later in the summer. Now, running two hundred yards wide, its current formed swirls and eddies as it rushed headlong toward the larger river a few miles distant. He had no way to know how deep it was. At best it was life-threatening to cross. If he was going to find Nate Niedermeyer, he had no choice. By his best guess, the pass that led into Foster's Hole was another five miles beyond the watercourse that barred his way.

He removed his gun belt and slung it over the saddle-horn, with the gun itself against the middle of the pommel. It would stay dry unless his horse went clear under. He pulled his hat down tight, as if about to fork a bronc. He touched the horse with his spurs, urging it into the rushing maelstrom.

If he had been riding Felicity, he would have been much more confident. In addition to her other attributes, she was an amazingly strong swimmer. The big gelding he rode was a good horse, but he had never ridden him before. He knew Brit Eisenbraugh had provided him one of their best horses, but it wasn't Felicity.

The animal stepped gingerly into the swift water. Finding firm ground beneath his hoofs, he perceptibly grew more confident. Even chest deep in the frigid water, he did not hesitate, even though the swift current threatened to carry him downstream.

Then he stepped off into the channel

of the creek itself. Suddenly there was nothing beneath his hoofs but more rushing water. His ears flattened against his head. His nostrils flared. He began swimming furiously. It was instantly obvious he was not as strong a swimmer as Felicity.

Orrin slid out of the saddle, holding on to the saddle horn with one hand. With the other hand he held the reins, keeping the horse's head turned upstream, against his will. As long as the horse could remain afloat, and Orrin could keep him angling upstream, the force of the current would push them toward the other shore as well as downstream.

He thought they should be gaining enough for the horse to find footing beneath the water, when he completely panicked. He began to fight against the reins, to twist his head, to lunge instead of swim. Instantly the powerful current spun him around. Horse and man were propelled helplessly with the current. One terrified squeal issued from the animal's mouth.

Hanging on for all he was worth, Orrin fought to talk the frightened beast out of his panic mode. Several times he was plunged beneath the murky water, then up again, choking and gagging. He was numb with cold almost at once. He couldn't feel the saddle horn he maintained a deathlike grip on. He knew he and the horse were both minutes from death. They would quickly be too cold to fight the current, and be sucked under.

As they turned in one more of the countless spins, the horse's flailing hoofs struck something solid. Instantly he stretched for the sense of something stable. His front feet caught and held just long enough for his hind quarters to swing downstream. Once more angling upstream, the relentless push of the current had the effect of also pushing him toward more shallow water.

The terrified gelding made a desperate lunge, and found footing with all four feet. The water was still chest deep, rushing with almost irresistible force, but the feel of solid ground beneath him gave him the courage to once again try to obey his rider. Half swimming, half scrambling for whatever foothold he could find, he began to work his way forward.

With each step the pair reached better footing and more shallow water. Orrin slid back into the saddle, urging his mount to continue. He didn't need much encouragement. Desperate for dry ground, he surged forward in great lunges until he was past the rushing torrent.

Orrin slid from the saddle, hanging on to it with both hands to keep from falling. He drew in deep gasps of air, then started coughing. In the middle of a fit of coughing he abruptly threw up a large amount of still icy cold water. He coughed some more, gasping for air.

He repeated the same procedure twice more. By the time he regained a measure of stability, the horse's sides had reduced their heaving as well. He shook himself vigorously, spraying Orrin with water.

He looked around. A thick stand of timber offered cover, to provide him with time to think. He knew he was still about five miles from the pass into Foster's Hole. He had at least a couple hours of daylight. Even so, the air was taking on the afternoon chill quickly. He was shivering so hard his teeth were chattering. He knew his horse was just as cold.

He mounted up and urged the horse into the timber. Four hundred yards into the trees, he found a small glade. One side of the glade was still drifted deeply with snow. The other side, where the sun hit directly over the tops of the trees, was bare and comparatively dry. He stepped from the saddle.

Leaving the horse standing with the reins dragging, he gathered wood from the top of a dead-fall that was dry enough to burn without smoking. From a saddle-bag he pulled out a square of wax. With his knife he peeled wax away from a couple of the matches that were sealed within, and started a fire.

Standing close enough to benefit from the fire's heat, he stripped off the saddle and rubbed the horse down as best he could. By the time he finished, the animal was comfortable enough to begin grabbing mouthfuls of grass. Orrin hobbled his front feet, and turned to his own needs. At once the animal walked off a short ways, shook himself again, then began to roll in the dry grass that remained from the previous summer.

Orrin stripped off his clothes. He wrung as much water as he could out of a wool blanket from his bedroll. He wrapped himself in it, mindful that the wool would keep him warm even when it was wet. He squeezed the water out of his clothes as best he could, then propped them up around the fire with sticks, so they would dry.

He made himself a pot of coffee, and drank the first cup of it greedily. By the time he was finished with it, he was feeling appreciably warmer.

'We pert neart bought it that time, didn't we, horse?' he asked the now grazing mount. The horse raised a head and looked, at the sound of his voice, then went back to tearing at the grass. 'I'll bet you ain't gonna go to the crick to drink for a while,' Orrin offered.

The horse was unaffected by the humour.

The dried biscuits wrapped in oilskin in his saddle-bag were only slightly soggy. The jerky was too dry and hard to begin with, to be affected by its adventure. Together they made do for his supper.

When he had dried the materials to be able to do so, he carefully cleaned and oiled both his pistol and rifle. He dried the cartridges with which he reloaded them, hoping no water had found its way to the powder. He wouldn't know for sure whether that was the case until he needed to fire one. He certainly wasn't going to fire either one just to find out, and draw attention to his presence.

By the time it was fully dark he was dressed again, in clothes that were more or less dry. Moving away from the fire, into the edge of the timber, he wrapped himself in a couple still-wet blankets, leaned against the base of a tree, pushed his not-so-dry hat to the back of his head to cushion him against the rough bark, and went to sleep. It wasn't the best night's sleep he had ever had.

12

His stomach knotted. He took a long, deep breath, exhaling slowly. He willed the tension to ooze away from his body. He wasn't very successful.

He studied the lay of the land before him. It was uncompromisingly devoid of good choices.

'The best choice is turn around and ride back the way I came,' he muttered.

From the cover of timber, Orrin studied the narrow defile. Crow Creek, like every other watercourse in the area, was running full and fast with spring runoff. A broad trail ran beside the stream, high enough to be above even high-water periods. It offered a simple and easy path into the valley he knew lay beyond. He had also been warned multiple times that it was pure suicide to travel it.

From high above that road, on both

sides of the rocky defile, he was certain there would always be sentries on duty. He had learned enough from the local cowboys, as well as the Eisenbraugh family, to be absolutely sure of that.

But where would they be? Their location would be dictated by both a clear field of fire on to the road itself, and by relatively easy access from within the valley. With someone always assigned to watch the approach, guards would have to be changed regularly. Even if they were organized with military precision, it would be difficult to enforce a sentry duty schedule if it entailed a difficult approach to the vantage points.

Orrin leaned against a tree and watched the sides of the defile for a long while. Large areas of randomly scattered boulders and scree were interspersed with clumps of cedar. There were pine trees, sometimes in lone isolation, sometimes grouped in ragged copses. Patches of brush clung tenaciously to any spot where enough dirt had accumulated to provide their roots some meagre foothold. Above the steep slope of jumbled rocks and vegetation, steep cliffs reared fifty feet or more at their lowest levels.

'If I climb clear up to the top and go past 'em, there ain't no way to get back down into the valley,' he muttered to himself.

The day was still and warm. The welcome sun had finished the half-done job of drying his clothes that his camp-fire hadn't been provided time to complete. Except his boots. His feet were still both wet and cold. His bedroll was still wet as well, but he wasn't overly concerned about that at the moment.

His eyes snapped upward to a spot on the right slope above the road. Something had drawn his attention, but he could see nothing. He watched carefully, then he saw it again. A wisp of smoke appeared for a brief moment before the light breeze dispersed it.

'Aha!' he said aloud. 'There's one.'

He continued to watch the spot, looking away then back again regularly. He was fully aware that if he stared at the same spot without looking away, he would begin to see movement where there was none. Over the top of one huge boulder, amid a cluster of others like it, and in a defile formed by the rounded tops of two other boulders, he finally spotted a hat.

'Now if he'da just wore a black hat instead o' one the same colour as the rocks, I'd have seen him a long time ago,' he complained to nobody but himself.

He turned his attention to the other side of the gap. Concentrating on a spot almost straight across from the sentry he had located, he finally spotted the other sentry. The ground rose sharply from the river, which ran parallel to the road. Fifteen or twenty feet from the river, the other sentinel occupied a well-worn patch of ground. He was sitting on the ground with his back against the trunk of a huge pine tree.

He was making no real effort to remain hidden. He was simply difficult to see in the shadow of the tree. He had a clear view of the road leading up into the narrow defile.

Orrin turned his attention to the area above each of the lookout posts. The slope on his left was almost totally devoid of any cover above the watchman. Not only would any attempt to sneak past above him be noticed by him, it would be clearly visible to the picket on the other side of the defile.

He studied the area to his right. The slope on that side held much more vegetation. If he were careful enough, he just might be able to get past above the sentinel without being seen by the sentry on either side.

The thought of that much walking reawakened his awareness of the lingering pain in his feet and legs. The walk to the Eisenbraugh ranch had left him sore enough it was still a chore to walk at all, let alone that far. Even if he could do so, his boots would almost certainly make enough noise at some point to betray his presence to the sentry.

Abruptly, he remembered the presence in his saddlebag of the moccasins Lora Lee's brother had so mysteriously given him. He felt the breath go out of him.

'Do you s'pose that danged kid has been in that valley?' he breathed to himself. 'If he has, he'd know I'd need 'em to get past the guards. Why would he go sneakin' in there anyway?'

Frowning, he turned back to where he had left his horse. He led him to a spot of good grass, where he could reach a large puddle of snow melt for water, and picketed him. He reached into a saddle-bag and drew out the moccasins. Replacing his boots with them, they felt remarkably good on his feet. 'What d'ya know?' he marvelled. 'I wonder if that kid made 'em hisself? He's just plumb full o' surprises.'

He had no idea how true that statement would prove to be.

13

Orrin had forgotten how good moccasins felt on his feet. The difference in heel height alone caused the sharp, nagging pain in the backs of his knees to disappear. He quickly remembered the old, nearly forgotten skill of placing each foot down carefully, so he could feel what was beneath it, before he put his weight on it. That allowed him to avoid breaking a dry twig, displacing a small rock to bound down the steep slope, or make any noise with his footsteps themselves.

Orrin climbed as far as he could in the ever-thinning timber. Where the scree met the vertical cliff, he began to move forward. As he took each step, he essayed the presence of both sentinels, measuring whether he would be in their line of sight, before he took the next step.

Close to that vertical wall of stone were more large boulders than he had realized. He was able to work his way around them without exposing himself to those below or across the chasm. At times, he went to hands and knees and crawled behind scraggly brush. For a-ways he was able to follow a narrow deer trail where he was able to walk, bent over, without being visible.

Then he came to an open area with no cover whatsoever. For thirty yards there was absolutely nothing to conceal his presence. Once he stepped into the open, he would be plainly visible to anyone who glanced up at the side of the canyon.

Across the gap, up the slope a-ways from the rushing mountain stream and the road beside it, he could see the guard on the left side of the road, still seated under the big pine. His head was tilted forward. Orrin thought his posture indicated that he had fallen asleep, but he couldn't be sure at that distance.

Below him, almost even with his position, the other guard leaned against a boulder, watching the road below. As if without a care in the world, the sentry began to roll himself a smoke.

Fearful that the slightest sound would direct the guard's attention upward, Orrin moved slowly, carefully forward. He also resisted watching the lookouts, well aware that most people have some kind of sixth sense that feels another's stare, even if asleep. Halfway across the clear space, his foot dislodged a pebble half the size of his fist. It started to roll downward.

Desperately, Orrin dropped to his knees. He lunged forward, with one hand on the ground to catch his balance. He clapped the other hand over the rock just as it was poised to roll over the top of a rock.

He looked quickly at the guard, no more than twenty yards away. The man took a drag on his cigarette and blew the smoke out in a long, slow plume. Carefully, Orrin moved the rock to a stable spot, then stood again. He continued, step by careful step, across the open stretch. Just beyond it, he stepped into a small stand of pine trees, clinging stubbornly to the steep, rocky side of the slash time and water had made through the mountain. Just inside their shelter, he turned and looked at both guards again. Neither showed any alarm or indication that they were in any way alerted.

It only dawned on him at that moment that he hadn't needed the amount of stealth he had employed. The noise of the river, rushing and tumbling over rocks and boulders, swirling in swirls and eddies, made enough noise he could have stomped across the opening in hobnailed boots without being heard.

Why then, he wondered, did Flint think he would need the moccasins? That worried him. At least he was past the guards.

Breathing more easily, he moved through the stand of hard pines. As they grew closer together, he worked his way downhill. From his position he could see the approach paths to both sentry posts. The guards needed only to walk a dozen yards from the road, along a wellworn path, to their assigned watch posts. On the river side of the road a great tree had been felled across the river. The bark was nearly worn from the top side of it by regular passing of sentinels to and from their post. Their location was ideal. Because of the road's steady rise as it followed the river, the stretch of road they monitored was then quite a-ways below them.

Both men's horses stood saddled, waiting for their riders' shifts of guard duty to be finished. Like cowpokes everywhere, even outlaws spurned any idea of walking half a mile instead of saddling their horse and riding.

Moving swiftly, staying far enough from the edge of the road to duck into cover if need be, he moved past the curve of the broad trail. The whole of the hidden valley came into view. He stopped dead in his tracks. His mouth hung open. He forgot to breathe until his body demanded he inhale a great gulp of air.

Before him lay the most beautiful valley he had ever seen. Nearly five miles long and almost as wide, it looked like a veritable Garden of Eden. Already spring was in full bloom in the sheltered haven. Green grass was everywhere. Wild flowers in prolific profusion of colours carpeted vast areas. Cottonwood, ash and willow trees grew along the river. Away from the water's edge copses of aspen, pine, cedar and spruce painted varied splashes of green. Beyond the far end of the valley, increasingly high ridges of mountains culminated in snow covered giants of granite.

Half a dozen log houses were visible from where he stood. A couple of them were scarcely more than cabins. The others were houses that would have graced any ranch. Each had a barn of one sort or another to shelter animals.

As he watched, a woman stepped out of one of the houses and vigorously shook a small rug. A child two or three years old stood close beside her, and followed her back inside.

'They even got their families in here!' he marvelled.

A large house dominated the scene. It was easily three times the size of any of the others. It had a roofed porch that ran along the whole front. Half a dozen steps in front of its front door a large bell, such as a church or a school house might boast, hung from a sturdy frame. A heavy metal rod lay on top of the crossbeam of the frame.

Near one end of the large house, a square log building sat with small windows at the top of the walls. Its purpose was not immediately evident.

One long building had the look of a bunkhouse. He reasoned it probably served the same purpose as the bunkhouse on any ranch. Men who came and went needed a place to stay.

It was provided for them in stunning style.

Several large tents appeared more or less permanent as well. Most had stove pipes jutting through the top, with tendrils of smoke drifting upward until the prevailing winds snatched them away. Every dwelling had a stack of cordwood piled within easy carrying distance.

A huge cottonwood that stood by itself had a limb from which the bark was nearly stripped in a broad circle around it. Beneath it, blood-blackened soil attested to its use as a place where the residents' meat was butchered and parcelled out on a regular basis.

Two dozen head of cattle ate placidly in the plentiful forage, wearing a variety of brands.

'They got a whole town in here!' Orrin marvelled.

Beyond the guards at the entrance to the idyllic vale, there was no sign of any precautions against attack.

'They're as 'snug as a bug in a rug','

Orrin remembered Brit saying. 'At the first warning of anyone comin' up the road, they'll all rush out there and take up positions in the rocks. They could hold off a whole army with a dozen men.'

They could also put a very sudden end to him, if his presence was detected.

Orrin moved silently through the brush and trees along the river, grateful now for the moccasins. He began wondering how he had any chance of finding his quarry, let alone taking him out of the valley undetected, and he struggled with whether to proceed or get back out of the valley while he could.

He remembered the crimes for which Niedermeyer was wanted — crimes that would be repeated many times over so long as the man roamed free.

His hand lifted to the side of his face where the still-tender reminders of the outlaw's attempt at murdering him in cold blood had filled his face with slivers. He held no illusions about whether he would try again.

He thought of Lora Lee and the proximity of the ranch to this den of vipers, and shuddered.

He remembered the sudden violence against the 'soiled dove' in the Silver Dollar, and marvelled that even that made him angry.

To leave the man lolling in leisure in such a place, without at least trying to arrest him, went against everything within him.

On the other hand, doing anything except getting his hind end out of there was tantamount to suicide, he scolded himself.

Orrin stood in the cover of the trees, fraught with indecision. In a stranger twist of fate than he could have ever imagined, Nate Niedermeyer walked out the door of the building Orrin had identified as a bunkhouse. He walked around the end of the building to the outhouse, twenty feet behind it. He stepped inside and closed the door.

Heart hammering at the unexpected opportunity, Orrin moved as rapidly as he could through the cover to the side of the outhouse. He looked around. There were no windows in the back side of the bunkhouse. Because of its location behind the long building, the outhouse was hidden from the view of anyone in the settlement.

He drew his pistol. He stepped to the door and jerked it open. He stepped inside. Niedermeyer started to announce the place was already in use. His eyes widened in startled disbelief as he recognized who it was. He tried to leap for the door. Pants and gun belt around his ankles tripped him up. He fell headlong out of the outhouse, on to the ground. Orrin leaped after him. The outlaw clawed amongst his wadded pants for his gun. Orrin's gun thwacked heavily against the side of his head. He dropped to the ground, unconscious.

Orrin untangled the outlaw's gun from the jumbled cloth of his trousers. Watching the supine man carefully, he shucked the shells out of his own pistol and replaced them with those from Niedermeyer's gun. 'Just in case. His ain't apt to've gotten all wet,' he muttered.

He pocketed the cartridges from his own gun belt and shoved them in his trouser pocket. He replaced them with Niedermeyer's. He started to toss the empty gun belt aside, then thought better of it.

He kicked the prostrate man in the feet. He groaned. He kicked him again. Some instinct told him the man had regained consciousness, but feigned otherwise to gain an advantage. He took a quick step back. 'Get up or I'll rap you up-side the head again,' he ordered.

Nate groaned again. He worked to get his feet under him, as if struggling to know where he was. When he had his feet positioned where he wanted them, he lunged for the bounty hunter. Once again the pants around his ankles betrayed him. He repeated his ignominious sprawl on the ground.

'Get up an' get your pants on,' Orrin ordered.

Slowly, with unfeigned difficulty, the hardcase struggled to his feet. He pulled his pants up and fastened them. No sooner had he done so than his nemesis whacked him alongside the head again. He dropped to his knees with a moan. Moving swiftly, Orrin holstered his gun and whipped out a pigging string from a coat pocket. He quickly bound the outlaw's hands behind him, and stepped back again.

It took the battered bandit only a few minutes to regain his feet, cursing profusely. 'You're crazier'n a pet coon,' he growled. 'You ain't got a snowball's chance in hell o' gettin' outa here alive, let alone gettin' me outa here.'

'Well, I've been thinkin' about that,' Orrin acknowledged, in a tone that would have been more apropos to a discussion of the winter's snow or the price of calves this year. 'But you see, it's this way. Either you keep quiet and come with me peaceful like, or I'll just rap you up-side the head again and take your head back with me in a gunny sack. The reward money's the same either way, an' that's all I care about.'

He knew the lie would fit the outlaw's mind-set perfectly. It was exactly what he would do, if their roles were reversed, so he would assume Orrin operated with the same philosophy. Nate's eyes widened for an instant, then narrowed to mere slits. He studied his captor, clearly trying to determine whether he would carry through with the threat.

He stuck the brigand's gun, that he had reloaded with his own cartridges, into his belt. He slung the man's empty belt and holster over his shoulder. He prodded him with his gun barrel. 'Let's go. Into the brush there, and walk right along the river. If I get the idea you're even thinkin' about tryin' anything, I'll rap that sore spot on your head again and cut your head off while you're out.'

Growling a low rumble in unaccustomed fear and frustration, the outlaw began to comply. They had made almost a hundred yards when the door of the bunkhouse slammed. A voice called, 'Hey Nate. Did you fall in out there?'

Nate slowed and turned his head as if to answer. Orrin jabbed him hard with his gun barrel. 'Don't even think about it,' he warned. 'Just keep movin'.'

Behind them another voice called out, 'What's he doin' out there, Morgan?'

Seconds seemed like hours before the answer came. 'He ain't here!' the one called Morgan called back.

'Where'd he go?'

If an alarm was raised now, he would have no chance whatsoever of escaping the secluded valley, let alone taking his prisoner with him.

'How do I know? I ain't his ma. I just wanted him outa the john so I could use it.'

Orrin breathed a silent sigh of relief.

Even so, he knew the respite from pursuit could only be brief at best.

'Well, don't take all day,' the one at the bunkhouse called. 'There's others that'd sorta like to use it sometime today.'

'How come everybody wants to go at the same time all the time? Just wait your turn.'

The sounds of the conversation faded as they moved further and further away. Once around the curve in the road, Orrin's attention turned to the two sentries they had to make their way past. They came to the guards' horses while they were still well out of sight of the pair. He shoved the outlaw to one of them. 'Climb on, cowboy,' he said softly. 'Let's go for a ride.'

With a murderous glare at his captor, the man complied. With another cord, Orrin quickly tied his already-bound hands to the saddle horn. Staying out of reach of any attempted kick, he loosed the lariat from the strap that held it to the saddle. He flipped the loop around

147

one foot, together with the stirrup, jerked it tight, and threw the rest of the rope under the horse. He sped around to the other side and grabbed it, while the bandit tried in vain to kick his foot loose from the noose. He looped the rope around the other foot and stirrup, and pulled them together. That bound both the man's feet and the stirrups close against the sides of the horse. It would make a very uncomfortable ride. It would also prevent any of half a dozen things the man might do to cause problems.

He walked the horse close to a tree and tied the reins to it. As if he could see the gears turning and grinding in the other's mind, he made a loop in the loose end of the lariat. He tossed it over the head of his captive, jerking it snug around his neck. That left more than twenty feet of rope unused. Orrin took the length of rope that was unused between the outlaw's feet and his neck, looped it around the tree trunk, and secured it with a half-hitch.

'Just in case you get the idea o' kickin' that horse enough to get 'im to bust the reins. If you do, and he starts to run, he'll bust your neck in a heartbeat. So sit nice and still and be plumb awful quiet. That horse sure looks to me like he's about to spook, if you make any noise.'

Retracing the path his entry into the valley had taken, he simply walked boldly up behind the sentry, leaning against the boulder and rapped him smartly above the ear with his gun barrel. He dropped to the ground silently.

'Shoulda used Niedermeyer's gun for that. I'm gonna bend my gun barrel if I keep this up,' he remonstrated himself.

He returned swiftly to the bound outlaw. The horse had, in fact, been fighting being tethered to the tree with the unaccustomed burden. The reins were nearly undone. Niedermeyer was quietly trying to soothe him out of the effort. The horse had moved far enough the noose was perceptibly tighter against his throat. Sweat was pouring from the bandit's face, contorted with fear. His eyes looked at his captor with silent pleading.

'First time he ain't cussed me out,' he told himself in silence.

Orrin pondered crossing the log bridge to take out the other guard. He decided he had already used up far too much time. The sentry he knocked out wouldn't remain unconscious long. If the other man was still asleep on his watch, they might be able to ride right past him, the noise of their passing masked by the noise of the river.

He mounted the second sentry's horse, jerked the half-hitched lariat loose, coiled the unused length of the rope, and dropped it over the outlaw's head to keep it from getting tangled around the horse's feet. He grabbed the reins of the captive's horse and started down the road at a brisk trot.

He could just as well have walked the horses, but he knew how punishing a good trot would be to the man tied tight to the saddle. 'Pay 'im back for a few o' them things he called me,' he rationalized.

He almost made it past the sleeping sentry unnoticed. He almost managed to pull it off. Almost. But in the words of an old hymn, 'Almost cannot avail; Almost is but to fail'.'

He failed.

Just as they drew abreast of him, the sentry woke. He jerked to his feet. 'What the . . . ?' he breathed.

It took no more than an instant for him to recognize that Nate was bound and being led out of the safe hold as a prisoner. He jerked his rifle to his shoulder. Orrin cursed himself for not being ready for that. He held the captive's reins with one hand and the reins of his own horse with the other. Even though he knew he was going to be far too slow, he grabbed both sets of reins with his left hand and reached for his pistol with his right. He never had a chance to complete his draw.

The guard flung his arms upward,

dropped his rifle, then fell forward. An arrow protruded from his back. Whoever shot the arrow was nowhere to be seen.

Simultaneously puzzled and extremely grateful, Orrin kicked the horse into a run, dragging the other animal along as well. They were well out of the gorge before a yell of alarm went up behind them. The first sentry, regaining consciousness, realized his companion was dead. Three shots were fired in rapid succession. They were too far around the curve and away to hear the responding yells from within the hidden settlement. He did hear the sudden clamouring of the bell he had seen in front of the largest house.

He knew pursuit would be fast. It would be furious. Almost as fast and furious as the raging torrent, he suddenly remembered they had to cross again. It had nearly drowned man and horse alike on the way in. He could figure out no way to cross it with a captive in tow. He was in as tight a box canyon as if he were in the centre of the outlaw enclave.

Nor did he know whether he might be about to be attacked by Indians as well. 'If my horse would just bust a leg too, life oughta get downright interesting,' he gritted.

14

His heart pounded in rhythm with the running hoofs of the horses. He tried desperately to think of a plan of action. He should have at least a fifteen to twenty minute head start. That wasn't going to be nearly enough. By the time the residents of the hidden glen realized what had happened, caught and saddled their horses, and launched a pursuit, he should at least be able to retrieve his own horse. What he would do then, he wasn't at all sure.

He just might take time to gag his prisoner, the first thing. The steady stream of profanity was laced with obscenities. Some of them Orrin wasn't even sure the meaning of. It was grating on him with increasing bile.

He caught up his borrowed gelding. He rigged a better lead rope so he could tether both his prisoner and the extra horse to his saddle horn. He replaced the moccasins with his boots. Hurriedly he mounted and rode out, forming a three-horse cavalcade. The entire stop took a little over ten minutes. 'So much for my lead,' he muttered. 'They're gonna be right on my heels any minute.'

He spurred his horse to a run, forcing the led mounts to do the same. The increased gait also increased the discomfort of the captive lashed so awkwardly in the saddle. His increased discomfort served to increase even more the vitriol of the promises of retribution he heaped on his captor.

More and more, the idea of simply taking the outlaw's head back in a gunny sack increased its appeal.

The horses covered a good bit of distance in a hurry. He hadn't yet heard sounds of the pursuit he knew was behind him. The river that he had nearly drowned trying to cross loomed suddenly before him. It was raging just as high and wild as it had been before.

His chances of making it across alive again was somewhere between slim and none. Less, even, than that, he decided, with three horses tied together.

He looked around desperately for a place to fort up and make a stand. Scattered forest was the only viable cover. He would be easily surrounded there. Then it would be just a matter of time before someone snuck in close enough to get a clear shot at him.

'Now whatcha gonna do, smart guy?' Niedermeyer sneered. 'I hope they don't shoot you straight away. I wanta kill you myself. Real slow.'

Caught in the throes of indecision, Orrin looked this way and that, fighting down the panic that surged up within him.

Abruptly a horse burst into sight fifty yards to his right. He whipped his rifle from its scabbard. With the gun almost to his shoulder, he recognized Lora Lee's brother, waving his arm. He was beckoning!

'Not there,' the youngster yelled, his

voice barely discernible over the roaring of the river. 'This way!'

He turned his horse upstream, kicking him into a run. With no other options, Orrin jammed the spurs to his own horse and followed.

He knew the pursuers from Foster's Hole would be following his tracks, clearly displayed in the soft earth where the frozen ground had thawed. They would know he was about to run right up against that uncrossable river. He guessed they would already have spread out to approach it in a wide half-circle, so they could close in on him from all sides. They would most likely slow down to do so, wary that he would be holed up and waiting to pick them off as they approached. If that were the case, and if he could cover enough ground quickly enough, he might make it outside that circle before it closed in. Then it would take them more time to find the tracks where he had turned upstream, and follow them. Depending on how slowly and carefully they approached where they assumed he was trapped, he might have a decent lead.

Flint led the way back away from the river, running as fast as their horses could in the alternating stretches of soft and still-frozen ground. Once over a rise, out of sight from where they had turned, he breathed a little easier. He knew the respite was temporary at best, though.

The youngster led the way down across a small ravine, its bottom running a goodly stream of snow melt. It was running fast and ice cold, but not too deep. They crossed it without trouble. The water was only half way to their horses' bellies. Up over a rise they found another shallow valley, likewise running with swift water that they managed to cross easily.

They crossed three more similar lesser watercourses before they came again to the main stream. As far as they had travelled upstream, and above the inflow of more than half a dozen contributing water sources, the river was dramatically less forbidding than where Orrin had crossed before.

Flint's horse plunged in and crossed at an angle, pointed upstream enough the current would help push them across. The gelding Orrin rode was from the same remuda as Flint's. He knew the horse ahead of him, so he followed without any excess urging. The two horses attached by the lead rope were visibly reluctant, but that tether gave them no choice. Once in the water, they surged toward the other side. The depth and speed of the water exerted enough force to nearly topple the horses, but they all managed to cross without having to swim.

When they were across, Flint motioned with his arm again. Orrin obediently followed, convinced now that the amazing boy knew what he was doing.

After crossing three more ravines that fed water into the raging flood tide of the river, he led them back toward its main course again. Beneath the brow of a hill, he slid from the back of his horse.

Whipping his rifle from its scabbard, he raced toward the top of the ridge with a quick, 'C'mon!' over his shoulder.

Grabbing his own rifle, Orrin scanned his prisoner with a quick glance to ensure that he was still secure. He followed the boy, who was now lying on the ground, peering over the top, his rifle in front of him.

Dropping to the ground, he crawled up beside him. As he stuck his head above the crest of the hill, a broad panorama opened before him. The river ran close in the foreground, just at the bottom of the hill they occupied. Well over two hundred yards wide, it carried trees, brush and debris with it, that lifted, turned and disappeared in the roiling cauldron, only to appear again downstream.

On the far side of the river, a band of horsemen followed the tracks they had left half an hour before. Flint's rifle barked. The front horse stumbled and went nose down to the ground. Its rider somersaulted over its head and hit the ground hard.

Following his lead, Orrin fired at the second rider. He misjudged the distance. His bullet kicked up dirt half a dozen feet short of his target.

The whole group of riders wheeled their horses and spurred away from the river, rushing to get out of range of the rifles they still hadn't spotted. Because nobody stopped to help him, the rider who had been flung from the downed horse scrambled to his feet and ran clumsily behind them. Another bullet from Orrin's rifle kicked up dirt just beside him. He somehow managed to begin running a lot faster.

'Stay down outa sight an' crawl back,' Flint ordered. 'Let 'em think we're still there. It'll take 'em long enough to figure out what we done that we'll be too far away for 'em to follow.'

He followed the youngster's orders, at once bemused and grateful that a lad not much more than half his age had assumed command.

As they remounted their horses, Orrin noticed for the first time the bow and arrows secured to the youngster's saddle. He opened his mouth to comment, but Flint was on his horse, kicking him furiously with moccasined feet, rushing away before he could get it said. He leaped into his own saddle and followed.

Five miles later the youngster reined in and allowed Orrin to ride alongside. 'Where to now?' Flint asked.

Orrin glanced at his prisoner again. The man was in obvious agony, swaying in the saddle. He knew the beating he had given the man hadn't hurt nearly as badly as having to ride that far, that fast, lashed to the horse as he was.

'Too far to try to get to town,' Orrin observed.

The boy nodded. 'We're on the main road. Too many tracks for 'em to tell where we went, even if they follow this far.'

'I doubt they will,' Orrin replied. 'Once they figure out they ain't gonna

162

catch us, they'll go back.'

'Old Man Potter'll rip 'em good,' the boy grinned.

'Who's Potter?'

'He's the boss in there. Emil Potter. He ain't so old, but that's what they call 'im. He's meaner'n a hydrophoby skunk with a cockle burr under 'is tail. Anybody crosses 'im, he just up an' kills 'em on the spot. He says who can come an' go, an' who can stay in there.'

Orrin was as stunned at the youngster's sudden loquaciousness as the knowledge he displayed. He didn't get a chance to ask about it. 'We'd best head home,' Flint advised. 'We got an empty grain bin we can stick him in till you're ready to take 'im to town.'

Without waiting for an answer, as if his own word were as binding as Old Man Potter's, the boy turned his horse and headed toward the L-Bar-E Ranch. With one eye on his suffering prisoner, Orrin followed.

15

'Thanks again for savin' my hide back there.'

There was no answer from the youth, who had returned to his taciturn nature.

After another long silence, Orrin asked, 'Where'd you come from, anyway?'

'When?'

'When I was trapped up against the river.'

Flint had said very little since they had gained the main road. Nearing the L-Bar-E, Orrin gave way to his curiosity.

The lad shrugged. 'I just seen you was runnin' the wrong way.'

'Are you the one that shot that guard?'

Silence hung heavy for another long while. 'Don't tell my pa. Please?'

'You saved my life. He'd have shot me before I could get my gun out.'

There was no answer.

'So how did you just happen to be there at just the right time?'

Again there was no answer.

After a long pause, Orrin said, 'I ain't tryin' to get you in trouble. I just didn't have any idea . . .'

He had given up hope of a response from the youngster, but he couldn't resist one more effort. 'Where'd you learn to shoot a bow and arrow?'

After only a short pause, Flint said, 'Running Elk.'

'Who's Running Elk?'

'He works for Pa. He's my friend.'

'Running Elk, huh?'

'Pateheya Nuki.'

'What?'

'Pateheya Nuki. That's his real name. Elk that runs. Running Elk. He's a Shoshoni.'

'Oh. Did he make the moccasins?'

'He taught me how. I made 'em.'

'You still didn't tell me why you just

happened to be there in time to keep me from gettin' shot.'

'Lora Lee told me to.'

'Lora Lee? Told you to do what?'

'Keep an eye on you. Not let nothin' happen to you. She's keen on you.'

Orrin's heart began to race suddenly. He pondered the significance of the statement. He hadn't been able to forget those eyes, or how she looked at him. That she was affected the same as he was a totally new experience for him. It caused emotions to surge within him that he had no idea how to deal with.

They were just coming into view of the L-Bar-E ranch yard. He turned to ask the youth another question. He wasn't there. He was simply gone. Orrin hadn't seen or heard him rein aside or turn off the road. It was as if he simply vanished into thin air.

He looked quickly at his prisoner. Niedermeyer rode slumped in the saddle, his chin riding on his chest. He appeared to be no more than barely conscious.

As the cavalcade shambled into the ranch yard, Brit Eisenbraugh walked out of the house. He yelled at the dogs to still their barking. Two more hands walked toward the house from the barn. A third stepped outside the corral and stopped, leaning against a post, watching and ready.

'I'll be doggoned!' Brit exclaimed. 'You actually got 'im, and made it back in one piece.'

Lora Lee interrupted, almost crowding her father out of the way. 'Orrin! You look awful! Are you all right?'

Feigning umbrage, Orrin said, 'Well, now I know I ain't no handsome dandy, but you don't need to tell me I'm awful lookin'.'

She giggled. 'I didn't. I said you look awful. There is a difference. Are you all right?'

He nodded. 'A little the worse for wear, but still in one piece. Brit, have you got a place we can pen this guy up till I rest up a day or two? It'll have to be awful snug.'

Brit nodded. 'We got one empty grain bin. It's built tight enough to be mouse-proof. There's a bar on the outside o' the door he sure ain't gonna bust by shovin' on it.'

Lora Lee spoke up. 'I'll go ahead and put some blankets and some food and water in it right away. That way you can leave him tied up till you lock him in.'

At the barn Orrin slid from the saddle. Rowdy Dawkins, one of the hands, untied Brit's gelding and led him into the barn to take care of him. Tubby Claussen — everyone just called him 'Tub' for short — reached a bone-thin arm for the lead rope on the horse occupied by Niedermeyer. 'We'd best leave 'im trussed up till we're ready to stick 'im in the grain bin,' Orrin advised.

Tub frowned. 'He's gotta need to relieve hisself after ridin' that far. I don't want 'im doin' it in the grain bin.'

Orrin's brow furrowed as well, as he weighed the risks against the decency of allowing him to do so before he was caged up. He glanced up and saw Brit approaching, a double barrelled shotgun cradled in the crook of his arm.

He looked up at the exhausted outlaw. 'I'll untie you, Nate. If you make one wrong move, you'll get a double dose o' buckshot besides everything I can pump into you. I still ain't too sure it wouldn't be easier to just haul your head into town.'

Fatigued as he was, the bandit looked daggers at his captor. Finally he nodded his head in silent assent.

Being careful to allow both Tub and Brit a clear line of fire if it were needed, he lifted the coiled loops off the outlaw's head and removed the noose from his neck. Then he untied his feet, allowing him to move them out of their cramped position against the sides of the horse. As they moved, a groan escaped the man's lips in spite of the fact his teeth were gritted tightly.

His bound hands were swollen from their long and unloving attachment to the saddle horn. He rubbed and flexed them, bringing feeling back into them. The return of that feeling wrung another groan from him.

'Climb down, an' keep your hands in plain sight,' Orrin ordered.

Niedermeyer slid out of the saddle, clinging to it for a long moment until his legs would support him. When he stepped away from the horse he staggered drunkenly. 'If you wanta relieve yourself, step around the corner o' the barn there,' Orrin said. 'Just don't forget you got three guns on you. One of 'em's a scattergun.'

Foregoing his usual litany of profanity, the gunman complied. The trio then herded him into the barn, frisked him carefully for a hideout weapon, and ordered him into the grain bin. Orrin noticed with satisfaction the canteen, a heaping plate of food, and a small stack of blankets.

The captor moved inside and they slammed the door. As he dropped the bar into place, Orrin looked over the device carefully. It was built to hold the door against the weight of a full bin of oats. There was no chance that anyone could force it open from within.

'The fill door on top good and secure?' he queried the ranchman.

Brit nodded. 'It's mouse tight too. The top's made outa planks to hold all the hay we wanta stack on top of it. The fill gate slides to open, so we can put the grain in. The pin that holds it shut is big enough he ain't gonna bust it. The hole there where we let the oats run out as we need 'em ain't much bigger'n his arm. Even if he got the gate lifted on it, he couldn't do nothin' but reach out a few inches.'

Mentally each man turned over in his mind the ways they could guard against his making any kind of escape attempt when they needed to replenish his food and water, or when nature called.

'There oughta be an easier way to make a livin',' Orrin admonished himself.

16

He liked the idea he had gleaned from the US marshal who had taken charge of Howard Dubray's return to Nebraska. He didn't have the leg irons or the chains the marshal had brought with him, but they made do with ropes. Niedermeyer was as securely hog-tied in the back of Eisenbraugh's buckboard as if the ropes were chains.

Brit Eisenbraugh drove the buckboard, with Rowdy Dawkins riding in the seat beside him. Rowdy was armed with Brit's shotgun as well as his own gun. Orrin rode directly behind, so he could keep an eye on the prisoner. Tub Claussen rode ahead of the buckboard. They all agreed the extra manpower was prudent, just in case some of Niedermeyer's cohorts were watching the road for a chance to rescue the outlaw.

The trip to town was notably uneventful. Marshal Clive Missner stepped out of his office in response to their arrival. He spat a brown stream into the dirt of the street. 'I've seen stage coaches carryin' a payroll that wasn't that well-armed,' he observed.

In short order, they transferred the fiercely defiant prisoner to a jail cell. The quartet gathered with the marshal in his office. 'You had him trussed up like you thought he was Samson or somethin',' Missner chided.

Orrin nodded grimly. 'Wasn't takin' any chances with 'im,' he replied.

'Bad customer, all right,' the marshal conceded. 'Now I got to deal with 'im.'

'We'll be lucky if he's the only one we'll have to deal with,' Brit opined.

The marshal looked at him sharply. 'Meanin' what?'

'Old Man Potter's gonna be hotter'n a forest fire,' Brit answered. 'That danged bounty hunter slipped into Foster's Hole, drug this polecat outa the outhouse, an' hauled 'im back to our place single-handed. That's somethin' Potter don't dare let anyone get away with. I got the boys all forted up at the ranch, lookin' after the womenfolk, on the chance they might hit there. It's more likely they'll come into town in force to get this sidewinder outa jail.'

Missner nodded. 'There's been a fella hangin' around the Silver Dollar the past few days. Nobody seems to know 'im, but he looks like a hardcase. I'm guessin' he'll be ridin' out inside an hour to let 'em know where this guy is.'

'I caught a glimpse of someone watchin' the road on the way in, too,' Orrin added. 'He likely decided we were too many for him to take on alone, but Potter prob'ly already knows we were bringin' 'im to town.'

Missner glared at the bounty hunter. 'You know, we was toleratin' that nest o' vipers up there, afore you showed up. It was some un-nervin', knowin' they was there, but we had things at a purty fair standoff. Now we're gonna have a war on our hands.'

'Had to happen sooner or later,' Rowdy offered. 'Just as well get it done with now as anytime.'

Missner chewed the ends of his moustache for a long moment. 'Well, I'll get a wire off to the governor. I'll ask him to send a troop from the fort. Hard to say whether he will, or how long it'll take.'

Brit responded. 'It's worth a try. If you need us, we'll be at the hotel. We'll let you worry about the town after tomorrow when we head back out home.'

It was the most relaxed night's sleep Orrin had enjoyed for too long. They were saddled up and the team hitched to the buckboard the next morning when Brit said, 'Someone's in a hurry.'

All eyes whipped to the road leading into town. A horseman approached at a full run. It was only a minute before Brit said, 'That's Flint! Somethin's happened.'

Missner had been standing with them as they prepared to leave. He swore and spat at the ground. By the time Flint slid his lathered horse to a stop before the group of men, several townspeople were either stepping outside or peering out of windows, frightened by the obvious alarm of the situation.

'Pa! Pa! They got Lora Lee!' Flint yelled as he leaped from his jaded horse.

Orrin's heart stopped. A vice clamped down on his chest. He couldn't breathe. He couldn't speak. He could do nothing but listen in stunned silence.

'Who's got Lora Lee?' Brit demanded.

'That bunch from the Hole!'

'What happened?'

Flint thrust a piece of paper at his father. 'They left this.'

Brit read the brief note.

It said, 'If you want to see the girl alive again, bring Nate to the gap. We'll trade.'

His face turned to stone. His eyes went flat and hard. He handed it to Missner. The marshal read it, handing it to Orrin. It passed around the group, each one reading it. Every face went pale. Lips drawn to thin lines, they all stared at Brit.

'What happened?' he demanded of his son once again.

'Ma hollered at me,' he said. 'Lora Lee went to the outhouse an' didn't come back in the house. She went out to look for her, an' this note was stuck in a crack in the outhouse. Runnin' Elk read the sign. He said someone grabbed her on the way back to the house. There was two of 'em, with an extra horse. They took her with 'em.'

Tears coursed down the youngster's face. 'I'm sorry, Pa! I was watchin' the road, but they didn't come thataway. I back-tracked 'em a-ways an' seen what way they took 'er. They went way around north, so's they wouldn't have to cross the river where it's high. I didn't think of 'em comin' around that way. I'm plumb sorry, Pa. What're we gonna do now?'

The group of men looked back and forth among themselves, each obviously hoping one of the others would offer an idea. Nobody did. The silence grew long.

It was Orrin who finally spoke. 'Flint. You know more about Foster's Hole than you been tellin'.'

The lad looked at him quickly. 'What d'ya mean?'

'When I asked if there was any other way in there, you almost said somethin'. Then you thought better of it. You've been in there a time or two, haven't you?'

The youth shot a fearful look at his father, then back at Orrin, then back at his father. 'I . . . there's . . . uh . . . '

'Time to spill it, Son,' Brit ordered.

Flint swallowed hard. He looked at Orrin. 'There's two other ways in an' out. Not on horseback. Just on foot. I don't think anyone in there knows about either one of 'em. Leastways, there ain't never been no sign o' anyone anywhere's close.'

'Anyone besides you know about 'em?'

'Just Runnin' Elk.'

'Can he slip in an' outa there without bein' seen?'

Flint nodded wordlessly.

Orrin took a deep breath. He looked around the group. His eyes settled finally on Missner. 'Clive, how many good men can you round up in a hurry?'

'From town, here? A dozen, at least. What're you thinkin'?'

Instead of answering, he turned to the rancher. 'Brit, how many can you gather up in a hurry from the other places close?'

'Between here an' home?'

'Yeah.'

The rancher thought a minute. 'Well, Farmington, from the Pegasus is a good man in a scrap. He's got three hands at least that'd be good. Don't know if they're close to the home place. Same goes for Samuel, at the Slash Box. By the time we get to the home place we could have another dozen.'

Orrin thought about it another long

moment. 'We can't wait for the army. We need to move before any scouts Potter has out can figure out what we're doing and sound the alarm.'

'What d'ya have in mind?' the rancher demanded. 'Remember, this is my daughter they've got up there in that hell hole.'

'Not for long,' Orrin promised fervently. 'I'll have her outa their hands an' safe before anything else happens.'

'How're you gonna do that?'

As Orrin began to lay out his plan, the rancher's eyes began to reflect a ray of hope beneath the burning flame of his wrath.

17

Twenty-six men rode out of the L-Bar-E ranch yard with the first streaks of dawn. A dozen of them were townsmen from Serenity. Four were from the Flying H ranch — the one most folks called Pegasus. Somebody had opined that the Flying H was meant to indicate a flying horse, which led to it being tagged The Pegasus Ranch.

Only two were from the L-Bar-E, besides Eisenbraugh. Brit insisted that four of his hands remain with Leah and Glen, in case the gang from Foster's Hole targeted them.

One hand from the Lazy H-2 ranch wore Nate Niedermeyer's clothing and Nate's hat, pulled low over his eyes. His name was Harvey Parmenter. He was nearly the same size as Niedermeyer. He rode hunched over, both hands on the saddle horn, as if they were tied there. His rifle scabbard and holster were empty. That his .45 was tucked into his belt beneath his coat, and that the rider on his left had a rifle in his saddle scabbard and a second across the pommel, was, they hoped, inconspicuous. If Foster had a look-out posted out away from the entrance to the hideout, they wanted to make it appear that they were bringing the outlaw for the swap Potter demanded. Only two men accompanied him, in hopes that the lookout would report only the two, and not hang around long enough to spot the rest of the posse.

Two other hands from the Lazy H-2 were in the main body. Two hands and the owner from the Double D, and two from the Lazy-8-4 made up the group.

They were a formidable, grim-faced collection of men. All were seasoned fighters, whether from the war, from the Indian wars, or from battling rustlers and horse thieves. They had lived in the shadow and fear of the growing gang in

Foster's Hole as long as they were going to do so. The kidnapping of a woman was the last straw. It was time for the Day of Reckoning.

They rode a wide circle to reach their destination, mindful they needed to use the same tactic Flint had used to get past the flooded river. It was close to noon when they gathered in a large tract of timber. They loosened the cinches on their horses and removed the bits from their mouths, so they could graze. Over several small fires, they made coffee and ate hardtack and cold side-pork. They waited.

Three men were not among them, who should have been. Orrin Reed, the bounty hunter, was conspicuous for his absence. So also was Brit's eldest son. Wishing for him the same strength and iron will as himself, the boy had been named Flint. Flint, son of Brittle. The other missing man was one who almost always went un-noticed. Unusual for one of his tribe, the Shoshone Indian named Pateheya Nuki — Running Elk

— was a working cowboy on the L-Bar-E. The success or failure of twenty-six deadly horsemen depended on the three.

Shortly after noon they tightened their cinches, packed away their things, and mounted up. Each man checked his guns for the last time. Each put a supply of extra ammunition in several pockets, to be sure they had plenty close at hand when it was needed.

'Hold to the timber,' Brit reminded them. 'Follow Lester, and be as quiet as you can. Les knows how close we can get without 'em bein' able to see us, even if they're watchin' with a glass. Just don't ride outa the timber into the open an' give us away.'

There were no more words said.

An hour later, at Lester's signal, they stopped. They dismounted. Each man stood at his horse's head, hand on the bridle. They waited. They worried. Some prayed. Some were convinced they didn't have a prayer.

18

'I have to go visit Mrs Murphy.'

The simple announcement shouldn't have sent the shivers of apprehension through Leah Eisenbraugh. It was nothing more than their usual euphemism for a visit to the outhouse, fifty feet or so behind the house. It was a long walk, it seemed in sub-zero temperatures, but it wasn't quite far enough during the heat of summer when it presented a harsh insult to the olfactory organs. Brit kept bags of lime on hand, and poured in a sufficient amount to reduce the odour on a regular basis, but it was still, after all, an outhouse. Since people became civilized enough to eschew any convenient spot in the brush, they have all smelled much the same.

Though indoor plumbing existed in larger cities, and had done so, apparently, as long ago as the time when

Abram left Ur of the Chaldeans, it was unheard of in Wyoming Territory, some thirty-six centuries later. Ranches or residences with families usually had a 'two-seater'. One of the seats was lower, with a smaller hole cut in the board that provided the sitting area, for the youngsters. The normal height was, of course, for the adults. 'The big-boy seat'. Or, 'Mrs Murphy's throne.'

As a result, the routine announcement of an imminent visit to 'Mrs Murphy,' or 'Mrs Jones,' or whatever happened to be the normal euphemism of the household, was simply part of the daily routine.

Some intuition caused that routine statement to ring alarm bells in Leah's mind. Her breath caught in her throat. Her heart skipped a beat. Perhaps some primordial mother instinct sensed a threat to her child she could neither explain nor ignore.

'Why don't you have Flint walk you out?'

'Mother! I'm not a child! I don't

need a nursemaid to take me by the hand to walk to the outhouse! Especially my brother!'

'But . . . your father said we should be extra careful out and about, since that . . . that bounty hunter you seem so fond of saw fit to bring that awful man to our place.'

'Well, he's not here now. They've already taken him to town, to jail where he belongs. So there's no reason to think any of his friends would come here.'

'It still wouldn't hurt to be extra careful.'

'Oh, Mother. Nobody from Foster's Hole is going to ride clear over here just to use our outhouse. It's perfectly safe.'

She donned her coat and flounced out of the house, more than mildly irritated at her mother's overly-protective fretting. It was dark, but she didn't need light to walk the path she had walked since she was out of diapers. Nor did she need to see her way around inside. The place certainly wasn't big enough to get lost in.

There had been a time she had carried a lantern with her on night-time trips. She had stepped into the structure once, several years ago, and been startled by the rattling of a large diamond-back rattlesnake, coiled in a corner. She screamed. Her father came running. He shot the invader. Nobody was hurt, nor in any real danger so long as they heeded the warning rattle. It amused her father to skin the large reptile and hang its hide, stretched, on the outhouse door. It had remained there for almost two years, before a windstorm ripped it loose and carried it who knows where.

So long as that reminder faced her on every trip, she had carried a lantern with her after dark. She used its light to check every corner of the edifice before stepping on in.

She was no longer a child, afraid of dark corners in an outhouse! The urging of her mother that she needed her brother — of all people — to walk her there, wait for her, then walk her back to the house was an insult to her maturity.

Her irritation had subsided by the time she stepped back outside. She turned the piece of wood on its nail that held the door shut when nobody was inside. She turned toward the lights of the house.

Without warning a hand clamped over her mouth. Another arm went around her shoulders. Her feet were lifted off the ground. She tried to scream, but the sound was so muffled by the large — and dirty-tasting — hand over her mouth that the sound was barely audible.

A coarse voice spoke softly in her ear. 'Shut up an' hold still! If you make any noise I'll slug you hard enough you won't wake up for an hour.'

Her eyes wide with surprise and terror, she stopped kicking her feet. The voice against her ear spoke again. 'I'll take my hand off your mouth if you promise to keep quiet. If you make any noise, and anyone pokes their head out the door o' the house, we'll kill 'em on the spot. You understand?'

The implications of that possibility penetrated the veil of fear that had shrouded her mind. She recognized she had no choice but to comply. She tried to nod her head, but the hand held her motionless.

The voice said, 'You gonna keep quiet?'

That grimy hand moved enough for her to mumble, 'Yes.'

The hand went away. A second man, barely visible in the darkness, walked past in front of her. He walked to the outhouse and stuffed a piece of paper in the crack between the door and its frame. White against the darkness, the note was sure to be seen by anyone coming to the outhouse to search for the missing woman.

'Get a move on,' the second man said softly. 'We ain't got much time.'

'Move!' the one who held Lora Lee ordered, giving her a shove.

She thought of trying to make a break for it. Run. Get away. Run and scream. Even as the thought entered her mind she knew she could never outrun the men, nor keep from tripping on something in the darkness. And if Flint, or anyone else, opened the door of the house, they would be perfectly illuminated by the light behind them, a perfect target.

Three horses stood patiently just inside the edge of the trees. The man holding on to her arm ordered, 'Get on.'

Once she was on a horse, maybe she would get a chance to escape. At the opportune moment, maybe she could rein away from the pair and flee. Since she was three years old she had been the talk of the family, and much of their neighbours, for her penchant for speed on a horse. Even at that age, riding bareback, she had loved to make her horse run. Constantly kicking and yelling at her mount, she could get incredible speed out of almost any horse, even at that age. It was never quite fast enough. She loved speed.

The plan was doused with ice water immediately. Her captors bound her hands to the saddle horn. Her horse didn't even have a bridle. It wore a halter instead. A rope ran from the ring of the halter to the saddle horn of one of her abductors. She would have no opportunity to escape.

With her positioned between the two men, they rode out slowly and quietly. Once well away from the ranch yard, they nudged the horses to a swift trot. With every mile they were farther from her home. With every mile Lora Lee's spirits sagged further.

Finally she worked up the courage to ask the question that was pounding at her mind. 'What do you want from me? Why are you kidnapping me?'

There was no answer.

Anger began to crowd down her initial shock and fear. 'Where are you taking me?'

The moon had risen over the crest of

the mountains, giving a soft light to the world, making their travel immensely easier. The men began to relax. One of them pointed at the moon. 'We just thought you might like to go for a nice moonlight ride.'

'Where are you taking me?'

'Ain't none o' your business.'

'It is my business! I'm the one being kidnapped. I have a right to know why.'

'Should we tell her, you reckon?'

'Why not?'

'OK. We're takin' you to the boss.'

'What boss?'

'Old Man Potter.'

'You mean at Foster's Hole?'

'You got it, lady.'

'Why?'

''Cause your people came an' kidnapped one of our guys. That wasn't a smart thing to do.'

'So what are you going to do with me?'

'Nothin', if your people come through like they oughta.'

'What do you mean?'

'We done left 'em a note. They bring Niedermeyer back to the Hole, still in one piece, an' we'll trade you for him, still in one piece. Simple swap. Nobody gets hurt.'

'What if they won't do it?'

'They ain't got much time to make up their minds. If they ain't got Niedermeyer there in three days, Potter's gonna let us boys have all the fun with you that we want.'

Lora Lee gasped at the implication. The sound was not lost on the outlaw. He chuckled. 'To tell the truth, I'm sorta hopin' they hang Nate. I never much liked 'im anyway. An' I'd trade him for the fun I can have with you in a heartbeat. It's been a long winter, holed up without a woman.'

Her heart sank clear to the slippers she wore instead of the boots she normally rode while riding. That her father would surrender the outlaw to rescue his daughter, she had no doubt. But it was not her father who controlled that decision. He was in the hands of the law. She didn't really know Clive Missner, except by sight, but she pictured him as stern, uncompromising, bound by principles that would prohibit him from capitulating to such blackmail, at any cost.

Orrin! Orrin would know what to do. She was certain the intensity of feelings she had developed so quickly for the bounty hunter was mutual. He loved her. She knew it. He had never said as much, but she knew it. A woman can certainly sense such things. He was almost super-human in his abilities. He would do something. But what?

Flint! Her omnipresent, protective little brother. He was more than a match for any man she knew. Well, with the probable exception of Orrin. He could literally sneak up on a grazing deer and slap it on the rump before it knew he was near. That was one of the 'tests' Running Elk had demanded he master. But there was no way for even him to get into Foster's Hole undetected. Or survive if he did. Or be able to rescue her, if he managed to survive long enough to find her.

Her mind continued to race, imagining scenarios in which someone might be able to figure out where she was being held, be able to reach her, be able to get her and themselves out alive. Every scenario she could improvise came full circle back to complete hopelessness. She had no hope.

Even as despair wrapped its dark cloak around her, the face of Orrin always broke through. He would think of something. He had to think of something! She had no other hope.

For the rest of the long, exhausting ride, she calmed her mind by thoughts of the man who had only so recently come into her life. From that first meeting of their eyes in Serenity, she had felt an inextricable intertwining of their lives. She couldn't explain it. She just knew, instantly, that this man held her future.

The fantasies into which she retreated sometimes made her smile faintly. Then a word from one of her captors, a stumble of her horse, some strange noise in the darkness would bring her crashing back to reality.

The first promise of dawn hinted of its imminent approach when they rode through the gap. The sentries were obviously aware of their coming. A few low words were exchanged as they rode past their sentinel posts. Then she got her first look at Foster's Hole.

She was dumbfounded. In the early light of morning, it looked more like Paradise than a haven for the off-scouring of society. Smoke rose from the chimneys of cabins and tents. Song birds revelled in the beginning of a new day. Crow Creek babbled merrily beside the road. A large, single-storey house quickly came into view. It would rival almost any ranch in the area. A small storage cabin stood near it. Beyond a little way was a rude barn and a cluster of corrals. Horses milled in two of the corrals. Three head of cows with new calves watched the approaching trio with mild interest from a third corral. One of the horses nickered a greeting that one of the outlaws' horses answered in kind.

Ringed about as far as she could see with steep cliffs, it appeared at once a secluded retreat from all that was threatening in the world, and an impenetrable prison from which there was no escape. Her churning emotions left her breathless.

Drawing rein in front of the door of the big house, the outlaws dismounted. One of them untied her hands and ordered her down from the horse. She obeyed without resistance. When she was two steps in front of the horse, the door of the house opened, and a man came out.

One of her captors said, 'Here's your pigeon, boss.'

Her first meeting with Old Man Potter was a shock. She knew that must be who it was who faced her. Her captor called him 'boss'. She had heard enough conversations to know the only 'boss' in Foster's Hole was Old Man Potter.

He might have been forty. Certainly no older than that. Only slight traces of gray coloured his temples. He was broad-shouldered, lean-hipped, with huge hands. He was clean shaven. He might have been any man she was likely to meet on the sidewalks of Serenity. In fact, she was almost sure she had done so, with no idea who he was.

He smiled, a disarming, open smile. 'Good morning, Miss Eisenbraugh,' he greeted her with smooth and polished language. 'I apologize for any discomfort you may have suffered in your journey here.'

She blinked in confusion. This was not at all the dirty, profane, infamous exemplar of evil she had imagined. Yet she knew full well the atrocities he had committed. That one that wicked could appear so carefree and wholesome flew in the face of every preconceived notion she possessed.

'It was not a ride I took by choice,'

she answered as quickly as she could garner her thoughts.

His smile broadened. 'No, I'm sure it wasn't. As I stated, I apologize for the necessity of that. I'm afraid our accommodations here will not be up to the standards you would choose, either. I apologize for those as well. Assuming your father and his friends prove reasonable, your visit with us should not be overly-long, however.'

Not thinking of an appropriate answer, she contented herself with staring silently at the outlaw leader. His smile abruptly disappeared. 'Put 'er in the shed,' he said, inclining his head toward the nearby cabin.

One of her captors again grabbed her by the arm just above the elbow and propelled her in that direction. He lifted the bolt from the loop in the metal hasp and opened the door. He motioned to the interior of the small building. When she hesitated an instant, he shoved her through the door. She sprawled on to the plank floor. She twisted to a sitting position just as the door slammed shut. She clearly heard the bolt drop back into its position.

It took a little bit for her eyes to adjust to the semi-darkness of the cabin. She stood up and essayed her surroundings. There were three windows. They were all small, right at the top of the walls. Around the small room supplies were stacked. Aside from them, it was empty.

Lora Lee sank down on a wooden case of something. She braced her elbows on her knees, cupping her face in her hands. Everything in her wanted to burst into tears of despair but she fought against it. She raised her head. She bit her lower lip. She would not cry! She would not beg! She would wait. She would pray. She would hope.

The bolt being lifted from the hasp seemed unnaturally loud. She leaped up and backed against the stored goods, as far from the door as she could. A stout Indian woman looked at her carefully, then entered. She allowed a bundle of blankets that she held between one arm and her side to fall on the floor. She set a bowl of something on the floor. She set a small canteen next to it. Without speaking, she backed out of the door and closed it. The bolt made a metallic snick as it dropped back into place.

Cautiously, Lora Lee picked up the bowl and smelled its contents. It smelled delicious! Stew! She sipped at the juice. The succulent flavour overcame any reservations she might have had. She drank the juice greedily, then picked up the pieces of meat and vegetables with her fingers and ate them quickly.

She removed the lid from the canteen and tasted it warily. It was cool water, from a well or the creek, she had no way to know. It tasted as fine as the stew, after her long ride.

With hunger and thirst slaked, she walked slowly around her makeshift cell. She examined the goods that were stored there, seeking something she could use as a weapon, as a tool to work her way out of there. Something. Anything.

The most encouraging thing she found was one loose board on a case of something. She worked and pried at it until she had wrenched it free. It was about two feet long, three inches wide, and an inch thick. Not the most effective club she had ever dreamed of, but it was something.

Exhaustion overcame her in a rush. She spread out the blankets the woman had brought and rolled in them. She lay awake a long time, alone in the semi-darkness, staring into the peril she knew she was mired in. 'Oh, Orrin! Please come to me!'

As she drifted into sleep, whether consciously or from some dream she was slipping into, she murmured, 'I love you, Orrin.'

The day went by relatively swiftly, since she slept much. She was given food and water again. She was led to the outhouse and back once, by the same Indian woman. She had no idea whether she was Potter's wife or a housekeeper. At least she was a good cook. That was something.

Darkness came. Everything seemed more bleak in the dark. She slept fitfully, fearfully, fighting against despair. The night crawled toward a new day of ever-growing threat.

With the first hint of light, the Indian woman came again. They made the routine trip to the outhouse and back. She stared at the bowl of what appeared to be the same stew she had eaten of twice before. She sighed and sat down on the same crate. 'Orrin, my love, please come!' she muttered as she picked up the bowl. Even as she said it, she knew she was asking the impossible.

19

The three-quarter moon rose over the mountain range to the east. It cast a deceptively peaceful, silver light to the earth beneath. It had none of the hard edges of daytime shadows. It had none of the harsh glare of the midday sun. It gave everything an illusion of softness, out of place in a hard land that teetered always on the razor edge of brutal violence.

Setting out in the first rays of that friendly moon, three grim-faced riders touched spurs to their mounts. A fourth horse, with an empty saddle, trailed behind on a lead rope. Two of the men were clad in the typical garb of cowboys. All wore filled cartridge belts and Colt .45 pistols. Each was sheltered by a heavy coat, collars turned up over knotted neckerchiefs, against the swiftly dropping temperatures of the early spring evening. With the morning sun, the temperatures would rise rapidly again, but the night air would be frigid.

The third man wore moccasins in contrast to the worn boots of the other two. He wore a neckerchief like the others, but had a smaller, flat-crowned hat. The hat sported twin eagle feathers attached to the hatband. His face was painted in garish strips of color. Those familiar with the customs of the Shoshone Indians would recognize it as war paint. They would also know the two eagle feathers had been earned in battle. He bore the appearance of a man caught between two worlds, yet able to embrace both equally, and formidable in either.

It was he who led the way. The other two were content to follow, knowing his knowledge of the land exceeded theirs. They rode in silence, maintaining the pace of a swift trot that steadily consumed the miles.

As they topped a rise, their passing surprised a mountain lion, feeding on a freshly killed deer. The fact that none of the three even reached for a rifle to dispatch the predator bore witness to their single-minded concentration on their mission. They were scarcely past when the feline slunk back out of the cover into which it had darted, and resumed its bloody feast.

They forded a dozen small rivulets of rushing ice-water, and one creek running bank-full. They knew if they had chosen a path farther downstream, those disparate small tributaries would be combined into one raging torrent. One of the three had nearly lost his life in that cascading current not two weeks past.

The silver moon had crossed two thirds of the sky when they dismounted at the leader's signal. They swiftly picketed their horses, loosening the cinches and hanging the bridles on the saddle horns. The two who wore boots replaced them with moccasins, almost identical to those worn by the one in war paint. One drew a rifle from its scabbard and filled his pockets with spare cartridges. The other two slung quivers of arrows on to their backs and carried bows of their own making. They looked at one another in silent query. One by one each nodded.

The lead was now assumed by the young one who had started out in cowboy garb. He seemed to have morphed almost into the image of the one adorned with war paint. The hat was the only thing that declared him not totally cut from the same cloth as the other. His moccasined feet trod as silently on the earth as if he floated just above it. He moved among trees and brush as though his passing touched no branch, snapped no twig, made no sound.

It seemed perfectly natural that the war-painted member of the party should glide like a silent shadow of the first. The third of the group was visibly all cowboy, except for the moccasins. Even so, he passed as silently as the other two, while not seeming nearly as much at ease in doing so.

As if rising out of the earth, a great yawning void emerged before them. The moon's glow clearly showed the far rim, nearly five miles away. They could see nothing of the rest of the valley from where they were.

Flint, the youth from the L-Bar-E, pointed silently. He began to follow the trace he had indicated, knowing the others would follow. A narrow deer trail led over the lip of the cliff that surrounded Foster's Hole. They kept to the track, knowing the deer would long ago have found and used the easiest path into the hidden valley. Flint followed it as if it were as familiar as the path from his house to the barn.

Sometimes the trail dropped into deep narrow defiles and up the other side. Not having the sharp hoofs of the deer, their moccasins didn't dig into the dirt for traction, so they had to walk carefully. Other times the trail led through thick brush, the narrow trail making only an inches-wide track to follow. Often they had to bend over into a low crouch to make themselves no taller than the deer who normally passed through the brushy tunnels.

Following the switchbacks of the game trail, they worked their way to the bottom of the broad valley. Flint, in the lead, picked up the pace. Keeping to the ample cover, they trotted in single file until they came into sight of the buildings. They huddled together.

'Where would they most likely be keeping her?' Orrin queried of the youth.

'Most prob'ly the cabin next to the big house,' Flint replied, speaking in the same hushed tones. 'It's set up for that. Potter'll wanta keep her where he can keep an eye on her, but locked up. That cabin don't seem to be used much. I think just for supplies. There's always stuff stacked in there. The windows is real small an' high up.'

'You been nosin' around in here a time or two, huh?'

The boy grinned, but didn't answer.

'Sun'll be up in half an hour,' he observed.

'Better to move while it's dark,' Running Elk offered.

Orrin shook his head. 'I don't wanta go bustin' into that cabin in the dark. We gotta wait till we can see what we're doin'.'

Light flared in a back window of the big house. It dimmed, then grew to a steady, yellow light. 'That's the kitchen. That'll be Potter's woman, startin' to fix breakfast,' Flint observed.

'She is Shoshone,' Running Elk stated.

'Potter's woman is a Shoshone?' Orrin asked.

Running Elk only nodded.

'How many women live in here?' Orrin demanded of Flint.

'Five or six. Four kids. All small. No kids in this house.'

'You have spent a lot o' time in here spyin' on them,' Orrin marvelled.

'It's where I've taught him how to be a Shoshone warrior,' Running Elk offered, an audible tone of pride in his voice.

'How many times have you come close to gettin' caught?'

Flint looked hard at him before he said, 'Couple times. Crawled under some brush and laid flat while they walked right past me once. I watched Potter kill one of 'em. Three of 'em were askin' him questions. They didn't like somethin' he'd done. They was talkin', plumb natural like. Potter was talkin' kindly, like he was best friends with the guy. He had one hand on his shoulder, smilin' at him. Then he up an' ran a knife I hadn't even seen into him. Shoved it in right under his ribs, pointed up, an' slashed sideways with it as it came back out, just quick as a wink. Blood come gushin' outa the guy like water out've of a pump. His eyes opened up real wide for a second. He grabbed hisself and looked down at all the blood on his hands. Then he fell over dead. Potter just said, 'Bury the garbage before it starts to stink',' an'

walked back in the house like nothin'
happened.'

Orrin watched the lad carefully as he
related the story, noting how he
trembled as he described the unknown
man's sudden death. 'Hard to watch a
man die, ain't it?'

'Yeah.'

'Somebody comin'!' Running Elk
whispered.

They all crouched down and backed
into the brush a little farther. The first
streaks of dawn were beginning to
soften the darkness the setting moon
had left behind. A stout woman with
long black hair walked out the back
door of the house. She carried a bowl
and a small canteen. She walked
directly to the small cabin.

They were not where they could see
the cabin's front door. They heard,
rather than saw, metal slide smoothly
against metal. Hinges squeaked as a
door opened. Muffled voices from
within were too faint to understand.

Lora Lee came out of the cabin,

closely followed by the other woman. She was escorted to the outhouse, some fifty feet to one side, back against the encroaching brush and timber. Orrin strained forward, readying himself to leap to her rescue. Running Elk's hand on his shoulder restrained him. He shook his head emphatically. Soundlessly he mouthed the words, 'Not yet'.

They kept their place and watched until the pair returned. The door of the small cabin shut. The sound of metal on metal repeated. The Indian woman walked back into the back door of the house.

Orrin looked at Running Elk, then at Flint. 'That Potter's woman?' he demanded.

Flint nodded.

'Took her breakfast.'

'Yeah.'

'Now what do we do?'

'Now we get her out,' Running Elk said.

The three crept to the corner of the cabin, on the side away from the house.

With hammering heart, Orrin noted that the cabin door would be clearly visible to anyone watching out of the house windows on this side. They could only hope nobody was.

He scanned the area in front of the house. It stood removed a goodly ways from the other cabins and the long bunkhouse. Smoke rising from beyond their sight indicated that those in tents were already beginning to stir and kindle their fires.

As if by some prior arrangement, Flint and Running Elk took up positions. At the end away from the house, Flint crouched at the cabin's front corner, watching the open ground. At the end closest to the big house, Running Elk crouched at the back corner, watching the back door of the house, or for anyone coming from that direction. Each had an arrow nocked in his bowstring, ready to respond to anything.

Orrin stood and walked boldly to the door of the cabin, as if he belonged there. With relief, he noted that the hasp locking the door from the outside was secured with a bolt dropped through the loop, rather than a padlock.

He lifted the bolt and swung the door quickly, hoping that moving it fast would prevent the hinges from squeaking. Most doors will squeak if they are opened or closed slowly. A goodly share of them will not, if opened quickly. He guessed right. It made very little noise.

In the dim rays of light that managed their way through the high windows, he saw Lora Lee, sitting on the floor. The bowl the woman had brought was in her hands. She was just bringing it to her mouth. She let out a small startled breath when the door jerked open. Her eyes opened wide in obvious fear, then focused on Orrin as he stepped swiftly inside.

With a stifled squeal she leaped to her feet. She dropped the bowl, rushed to him and flung her arms around his neck, hugging him as if in fear that he might melt away like a dream with unwilling wakefulness. She buried her head against his chest, then lifted her head, grabbed his face with both hands and began smothering him with kisses.

Torn between wanting the moment to last forever and the urgent need to get out of there, Orrin returned her embrace, then pushed her away. He placed a finger on her lips. 'Shhh!' he cautioned softly. 'We gotta get outa here.'

He took her by the hand and led her out the door, watching all around. He swiftly closed the door and dropped the bolt back into the loop of the hasp. Having fed her breakfast, he hoped her captors wouldn't bother with checking on her until time for her to be fed again.

They scurried around the corner where Flint crouched, watching. As they passed him, he rose and followed close behind. Hearing what Orrin thought was no noise at all, Running Elk rose and melted into the brush as well.

The quartet moved swiftly away from the house and cabin. As soon as they were far enough away to feel momentarily safe, Flint turned and looked his sister over carefully, from head to toe. 'You OK, Lora Lee?' he asked, the worry sharp in his voice.

She nodded her head, embarrassing the youth with a quick hug. 'I'm OK now,' she said. 'Little brother, you are an angel!'

She turned to Orrin, her eyes shining. 'I knew you'd come,' she said. 'I didn't know how or when, but I knew you'd come.'

'We ain't outa here yet,' Orrin cautioned.

'We gotta move quick now,' Running Elk urged. 'Just in case they miss her.'

They retraced the path by which they had entered the valley, moving swiftly but as silently and furtively as possible. Flint led them unerringly to where the deer trail began its ascent. They were a hundred yards along, beginning to climb rapidly, when Flint waved a frantic arm and ducked back into the brush at the side of the trail.

The others followed suit instantly. Only Running Elk seemed to know why they were hiding. He had an arrow nocked and ready, pointed toward the deer trail. It was seconds later they heard the voices.

'How long you known about this trail?'

'Just found it yesterday. Old Man Potter told me to check all the way around the rim, just in case. I almost didn't see it.'

'Ain't seen any tracks on it?'

'Just deer an' catamounts an' such. Doubt if anyone knows about it.'

'We'll leave Cletus hid up there just in case. He'll spot anyone comin' up or down thataway. I'll send Rafterty up to relieve him after noon.'

They passed the hidden quartet, moving down toward the valley. When they were gone, the group moved back on to the trail.

'Now what do we do?'

'We can go back down. Slip around

and go out by the road. We can take out the sentries again.'

That was the first Flint had acknowledged being the one who had killed the guard that was preparing to shoot Orrin.

'Too much chance o' bein' seen,' Orrin vetoed. 'If one of us is spotted, it'll blow up the whole rest o' the plan.'

'What plan?' Lora Lee demanded.

Orrin looked at the others for silent permission to bring her into the scheme. Each nodded almost imperceptibly.

'There's a couple dozen men on their way to the Hole. Ahead of 'em are two men that look like they're bringin' Niedermeyer to swap for you. We gotta be where we can take care o' the sentries while they're watchin' those three. Then the rest o' the bunch will ride into the Hole and surround everyone and clean house.'

Her eyes were wide and round. 'You mean they're just going to kill everyone?'

He shook his head. 'Not if they can help it. They'll try to get 'em to surrender instead. If they don't, there's gonna be a lotta lead flyin'.'

He turned back to the other two. 'If that guy at the top gets off a shot, it'll sure let 'em know somebody's comin' in this way. Then they'll look for Lora Lee, and figure out where we took her. It'll blow things up for sure.'

With a voice that was as quiet and low as a primordial death-wind, Running Elk said, 'He won't get off a shot.'

Flint gave his mentor a stare as hard as his name. 'We both go.'

The Shoshone looked with pride at his protégé. 'We both go,' he agreed.

Orrin looked at Lora Lee, then back at the pair. 'We'll tag along a-ways. When we're still well short of where he's likely to be, we'll hole up in the brush.'

Without another word they started back up the trail. This time Lora Lee's hand found his. She clung to him as to a lifeline in a stormy sea.

20

The silence closed around them. At irregular intervals, the slight noise of some small woodland creature carried to their ears. A young buck mule deer appeared on the deer trail. Soft fledgling antlers covered with velvet sprouted from his head. He walked along the trail for a dozen yards, then angled off into the brush. They could hear his departure for two or three minutes before the silence resumed its grip.

Lora Lee crouched tightly against Orrin. She maintained a tight grip on his arm until he moved it, and wrapped it around her shoulders. She snuggled more tightly against him. She shivered slightly. Realizing for the first time that she wore only a short coat, he unbuttoned his own and wrapped it around her, enfolding her against himself within its warmth.

Except for the discomfort and the danger of their situation, he would have willed for Flint and Running Elk to take a long time on their mission.

Muscles were beginning to cramp from lack of movement when the pair appeared as if by magic on the trail.

Both Orrin and Lora Lee jumped, startled when the pair suddenly appeared. They stood, looking at the duo with unspoken question.

Running Elk nodded. 'He ain't gonna set off no signal.'

Lora Lee looked up at Orrin. She still stood against him, still wrapped in his coat. The bounty hunter spoke. 'We gotta get our horses an' get around where we planned. We gotta be where we can take out the sentries while they're watchin' the one they think is Niedermeyer.'

'Then let's move,' Flint said, turning back up the trail.

They traversed the distance to their horses much faster than they had gone the other direction. As they approached, Lora Lee said, 'Oh! You brought my horse!'

Orrin grinned. 'I'd be plumb happy to have you ride double with me, but it might get uncomfortable after a while.'

The sun was high enough in the sky to be rapidly warming the earth. Lora Lee's sharing of Orrin's coat was no longer a need. It was, however, a very convenient excuse to stay close against him. Neither of them were making any effort to conceal their feelings for each other.

Removing the pickets from the horses, tightening the cinches, replacing the bridles, took only minutes. They mounted and rode at a gait that varied from a fast trot to a ground eating lope, depending on terrain. At one point, when they had ridden nearly an hour, Flint held up a hand and stopped them.

'I need to go up that draw. I can get in a spot where I can take care of the guard on this side easier than if I go on around with the rest of you.'

Confident of his knowledge of the approaches to the gap and his abilities, Orrin just nodded. The other three continued on. Another hour later they drew rein at Orrin's signal. 'We need to leave the horses here.'

Moving swiftly and silently, they followed the course Orrin had figured out on his way into the Hole after Niedermeyer. When they were close to the vantage point he sought, he spoke to Running Elk. 'About a hundred yards on up there's a spot where you can look right down on the guard on this side. Don't take him out until the others get here. Flint'll be waitin' for you to do somethin' afore he does. They'll think it's Niedermeyer they're bringin'. We need to let 'em get right up into the gap, so the ones followin' will get here in a hurry. They won't be far behind.'

Running Elk melted away into the brush and boulders at the base of the cliff.

Orrin leaned back against a tree. Lora Lee stepped in front of him and leaned back against him. He wrapped his arms around her. She leaned her head back against his chest. They stood that way for a long while. She whispered, 'Can we talk?'

He didn't whisper, but he kept his voice low. 'Yeah. Not loud. The guards are right above the crick. It makes noise enough this time o' year that they can't hear us from here.'

She tilted her head back and looked up at him. 'Do you know how I kept from panicking, while they had me locked up?'

'How?'

'Talking to you.'

'Talkin' to me?'

'I went to sleep talking to you, and woke up talking to you, even though I knew you couldn't hear me. I knew you would come for me. I didn't know how. I didn't know when. But I knew you wouldn't leave me there.'

After a brief silence he replied, 'I'd

have gotten you outa there or died tryin'.'

'It was while I was talking to you, all alone there, that I really realized that I love you.'

Again a silence ensued, slightly longer. His voice was husky as he said, 'I figured out how much I love you when your brother came whippin' into town to tell us you'd been took. I knew right then that I just couldn't live no more without you.'

She turned around in his arms and put her own arms around him. She tipped her face up to him. 'I love you, Orrin Reed.'

Their lips met for the first time. The world retreated to a discreet place away, allowing them the privacy of their moment. It didn't last long. Not nearly long enough for either of them.

Above the busy babbling of Crow Creek the words of one of the guards, calling out to the other, floated down to them. 'They're comin'. I can see 'em.'

'How many?'

'Three.'

'Nate one of 'em?'

'Yeah. Looks like 'im, anyway. He's kinda slouched down. That's his old beat-up hat for sure.'

'Who's with 'im?'

'Don't know 'em. Both ridin' L-Bar-E horses, though. One looks kinda like Eisenbraugh.'

'Yeah he does. I can see 'em now, too. Yeah, that sure enough looks like Nate.'

'Looks like his hands is tied to the saddle horn.'

'That makes sense. They ain't gonna take a chance on 'im gettin' away afore they get the girl.'

'Shall I go tell the boss they're here for the swap?'

'Not yet. Let 'em get right up here.'

Though neither Orrin nor Lora Lee could see, both guards stood up where the approaching riders could see them.

After just a few minutes one of the guards said, 'They're stoppin'.'

'Yeah. They ain't likely gonna get any

closer till they see the girl. They ain't dumb enough to ride clear on in here.'

'Bring the girl before we get any closer,' another voice, obviously one of the approaching horsemen, called.

'Shall I go tell the boss?'

'Yeah, I 'spect you better.'

'Hey, what's that? There's more men comin'!'

Grunts and thumps were impossible for Orrin and Lora Lee to interpret. The dreaded gunshots that would betray the plan didn't come. The first indication of what was going on came to them with the voice of Running Elk. 'The guards are took care of.'

'Come on,' Orrin said, grabbing Lora Lee's hand.

As they crashed through the brush on to the road they found themselves looking down the gun barrels of the two 'escorts' of the fake Niedermeyer.

Tub Claussen swore. 'You dang near got yourselves shot, bustin' outa the brush without announcin' yourselves first.'

Before Orrin had a chance to answer, the first of the posse rode out of the trees. They were leading the three horses that were left hidden while the trio had made their way to eliminate the guards.

Brit leaped from the saddle and ran forward to embrace his daughter. 'You OK, Nubbin'?' he demanded, using his pet name for his daughter. It was the first time Orrin had heard it.

'I'm fine, Father,' she returned his hug. 'I knew you'd come, or send Orrin. Or both.'

'What about me?' Flint demanded. Nobody had seen him emerge from the trees.

Lora Lee turned and impulsively hugged her brother. For once he didn't cringe away, but returned the hug. She stood back and said, 'With all three of you, all the outlaws in Foster's Hole didn't have a chance!'

'Which brings us to 'What do we do now?'' Harvey Parmenter demanded, taking his rifle that Tub handed to him, and moving his pistol from his belt to its holster.

As if by some pre-arrangement, all eyes turned to Orrin. He took charge as if it were the natural thing to do. 'We need to leave four men here. Two on each side o' the road. Up in the rocks, where you can see the road plain and have some cover. There's a log across the crick up a ways where the ones on that side can get across. One needs to stay with the horses. The rest of us need to go in on foot. Split in two bunches. Stay in cover and spread out so we'll have 'em from all sides. I'll holler for 'em to come out with their hands up, an' tell 'em they're surrounded. Be ready, but be careful. If we're all the way around 'em, shootin' at 'em will mean we're shootin' toward our own guys on the other side of 'em. Shoot low, especially if you ain't dead sure o' hittin' your target.'

Controlled chaos reigned for several minutes, as men turned back and tied their horses in the timber. Four men took the initiative to climb to posts above the road in the rocks, finding and occupying positions that provided clear view of the road as well as cover.

When everyone was ready, Brit said, 'Lora Lee, you stay with the horses.'

Her face turned crimson. Her lips thinned. Her eyes narrowed. 'I'm not hiding out with the horses while everyone else deals with those . . . those . . . '

'I ain't havin' you where you might catch a stray bullet or let 'em get a hold o' you again,' Brit declared, his voice as brittle as his name.

Lora Lee looked imploringly at Orrin. He shook his head. 'Much as I'd like to have you close, I can't do what I gotta do if I'm worried about protectin' you at the same time.'

Running Elk extended a rifle to her. 'Take the guard's gun with you. Just in case you need it, or someone gets past the guys in the rocks. Make sure the horses don't spook.'

As a last resort her eyes whipped

around to her brother. Flint found it necessary to study his moccasins intently. She stomped a foot, raising a small cloud of dust. In spite of her umbrage, she knew they were right. She whirled and trounced to where the horses were tied.

'Let's do it, afore we run outa daylight,' Orrin said.

Moving swiftly, they traversed the defile. Just before they would come into view of the valley and its occupants, Orrin signalled them to split up and move into the cover. Running Elk took it upon himself to take the lead of the group on one side. Orrin allowed Flint to move ahead of him, taking the lead on the other.

When he decided everyone had ample time to get into position, Orrin stood beside a tree at the edge of the timber, a hundred feet from the front of the big house. 'Potter!' he bellowed. 'You and your men are surrounded. Throw up your hands and come out.'

His words carried clearly to every

corner of the valley, bouncing off the high cliffs in endless repetition. Deathly silence followed. It was followed seconds later by pandemonium.

The Indian woman broke from the front door of the house. She raced to the big bell, grabbed the steel rod and began banging on it furiously. The pealing of the call to battle drowned out all other sound as it bounced from the cliffs.

At the same time that she burst through the front door, Potter flew out the back door. He ran to the small building where Lora Lee had been held captive. He flipped the bolt from the hasp and jerked open the door. He stopped dead in his tracks, staring in disbelief at the empty chamber he had thought held his ace in the hole.

From all around the settlement men had poured out of cabins, tents and the bunkhouse, guns blazing at any hint of movement. Rifles responded from trees and brush.

Orrin yelled at the outlaw leader.

'Give it up, Potter! You're finished. Throw up your hands.'

Potter spotted him as he began to speak. He whipped out twin .45s and began firing. He fired one at a time, first with one hand then the other. As he drew the weapons, Orrin ducked back behind the tree. Bark flew in all directions.

Orrin dropped to the ground. He raised up enough to see the outlaw racing toward him, firing as he came. Staying below the man's line of fire, he raised his rifle and fired. Potter hesitated for the barest moment, then started forward again. Orrin fired again. Potter stopped in his tracks. He spotted his opponent. He pointed one of his pistols at Orrin and squeezed the trigger. The hammer fell on a spent chamber.

Swearing, Potter flung the gun away and grabbed another that was tucked under his belt. Orrin fired again.

Potter lifted the pistol, intent on at least taking his enemy with him if he must die. A bullet from his left side slammed into him at the same time as Orrin's fourth round found its mark. They drove the would-be king of Foster's Hole into permanent exile. He was dead when he hit the ground.

The woman, who might have been his wife, who might have been a house-keeper, who might have been whatever she chose to be, burst back out of the house, a rifle in her hands. She began firing at Orrin, the bullets whizzing close enough he could hear the whine of their passing. Orrin aimed his own rifle at her, but couldn't pull the trigger.

He hadn't realized that the gunfire had ceased all around the settlement until a lone rifle barked. The woman staggered a step and went down.

Silence returned to the valley. Three men stood in the open, their hands in the air. A cabin door opened. A woman's voice shouted, 'Don't shoot!'

An instant later a woman appeared. Two small children stayed huddled close to her as she walked out, hands in the air.

Orrin barked, 'Anyone still inside, come on out with your hands up.'

A moment later three more women emerged, then a fifth. Together they brought three more children, ranging from one baby to a girl of ten or eleven.

Somebody began to move from tent to tent, setting fire to the flimsy shelters. Someone else picked up on the idea and set fire to a couple of the small cabins.

When one of them approached the big house, Orrin intervened. 'Not that one. Check it out. Make sure there's nobody inside. But don't burn the other houses or the barns or the bunkhouse.'

The men of the posse, who had moved cautiously out of their cover looked at him inquisitively. 'This place'll make a fine ranch for someone,' Orrin announced. 'No sense burnin' what don't need burned.'

It didn't occur to anyone at that moment to ask whether he knew who that someone might be.

Epilogue

When the icy grip of winter drives hardy souls indoors, all unnecessary work grinds to a halt. Cattle and horses are fed. If necessary, ice is broken for them to drink. By mid-afternoon it's time to seek shelter. When the frigid winds howl down from the mountains and those winter evenings wax long, folks tend to gather in small groups to share gossip, to commiserate, or just to chat.

In some places the talk flows more freely with the fluid that tends to loosen tongues. So it is in a town with the whimsical, hopeful name of Serenity. Then it is that they talk at the Silver Dollar saloon about a day, some years ago, when an era of lawlessness and fear was brought to an end in that country.

Details of a blazing gunfight between an entrenched gang of outlaws and a determined posse had been amplified, exaggerated and improved upon with each telling. It had taken on a mystique to rival any of the legends of yore. Nearly a hundred men now claimed to have been among the two dozen involved.

There was only one minor wound among the posse, they insisted. A miracle in itself. A woman hostage was rescued unharmed. Right out from under the outlaws' noses. The stuff of which legends are made.

Some claimed to remember the exact words of a Shoshone warrior, one of the posse, who straddled both worlds. He rode in the white man's posse, wearing the war paint of the Shoshone. It was he whose rifle brought down the Shoshone woman who, alone of the outlaws, continued to fight when all others were dead or surrendered. 'It was my duty,' he had said. 'She has disgraced my people.'

They told of the lucrative rewards a certain bounty hunter had gleaned from five who were killed, and one who had surrendered. He had tried to share those rewards with those who rode with him that fateful day. To a man they refused. It was an age of integrity, the old timers insisted, when credit belonged to the one who instigated and led the necessary action. They just went along, and did what had to be done.

Tongues clucked with a measure of sympathy for the women and children who had been loaded into a wagon per family, staked with a generous amount of the hidden loot their men had died trying to defend, and ordered to begin a new life somewhere far away from the town of Serenity.

In those intervening years most had forgotten — or chose not to remember — or to remind anyone — that the fabled bounty hunter had abandoned his chosen profession, married the girl of his dreams, and became one of the respected ranchers of the area.

They did mention, from time to time, that the brand V-Bar-E on the left hip

of a sizeable herd of cattle stood for
Valley of Eden Ranch.

For some, it had truly become the
Valley of Eden.

None of them ever did figure out
what a snizzle-biscuit was.

BULL'S EYE STAGE COACH
THE BRONC BUSTER
SAM AND THE SHERIFF
BLIND-SIDED

We do hope that you have enjoyed reading this large print book.

Did you know that all of our titles are available for purchase?

We publish a wide range of high quality large print books including:
**Romances, Mysteries, Classics
General Fiction
Non Fiction and Westerns**

Special interest titles available in large print are:
**The Little Oxford Dictionary
Music Book, Song Book
Hymn Book, Service Book**

Also available from us courtesy of Oxford University Press:
**Young Readers' Dictionary
(large print edition)
Young Readers' Thesaurus
(large print edition)**

For further information or a free brochure, please contact us at:
**Ulverscroft Large Print Books Ltd.,
The Green, Bradgate Road, Anstey,
Leicester, LE7 7FU, England.
Tel:** (00 44) **0116 236 4325**
Fax: (00 44) **0116 234 0205**

REINS OF SATAN

Lee Clinton

The reins of Satan are harnessed to the sins of violence . . . Civil War veteran Gabe McDermott has spent the last thirty years working as an enforcer for anyone who can pay. Desiring to escape his past and settle down, he turns in his young partner Hiram Miller for a $1,500 reward. However, when Hiram is hanged without a trial, the execution awakens Gabe's lost conscience. Memories from his former life return to haunt him, and his nerve fails — just when Satan decides to call . . .

THE TOMB OF IRON EYES

Rory Black

Infamous bounty hunter Iron Eyes has the scent of his prey in his nostrils, and is determined to add yet another notch to the gun grip of his famed Navy Colt. Yet the closer he gets to where his outlaw quarry is holed up, the more guns are turned upon him. Refusing to submit to the lethal lead of those who would halt his progress, Iron Eyes forges on towards Cheyenne Falls — and the fate that he knows awaits him . . .

THE BOUNTY MAN

Gordon Landsborough

Bounty hunter M'Grea is a big man, topping most of his fellows by several inches, and can hold his own with the best in a fight with fists — or guns. Now he has killers Dutch George and King Rattler in his hands — all that remains is to turn them in and and collect the bounties. But that isn't going to be easy: dangerous Apaches are very near, and the trio is about to walk into a deadly trap . . .

WILD WEST DETECTIVE

James Clay

Rance Dehner, an operative for the Lowrie Detective Agency, pursues a wanted killer to the small town of Hardin. After bringing down his opponent in a gunfight, Dehner discovers the man was in town to murder Leona Carson — a penniless teenaged girl with a baby. Seeking to discover why anyone would hire a gunman to dispose of Carson, Dehner finds himself dodging bullets from an onslaught of professional killers — whilst uncovering the shameful secrets of Hardin's leading citizens.

TOUGH JUSTICE

Colin Bainbridge

Burt Lowell lives as a recluse in an abandoned ghost town — until someone puts a price on his head. And Burt wants to find out who, and why. The trail leads to Ludwig Rickard, scheming owner of the Half-Box M, with his eye on the Long Rail. But there is a more sinister figure behind him: the elusive railroad boss Abbot Mossman. Somewhere down the tracks, Lowell must confront his would-be killer on his own ground . . .

DESERT RUN

Neil Hunter

Bodie is trailing a trio of escapees from Yuma Pen — three men he'd helped to put there in the first place. But when they shoot his horse out from under him, he finds himself adrift in the searing desert. If he's to turn the tables on those now hunting him, he needs to reach the life-saving waters at Pinto Wells. But there's another shock awaiting him. A face from his past. A man supposed to be dead. A killer who's tracked Bodie down, and plans to exact his own vengeance . . .